my
girlfriend's
boyfriend

my girlfriend's boyfriend

elodia **strain**

bonneville books
springville, utah

ISBN 13: 978-1-59955-905-6

Published by Bonneville Books, an imprint of Cedar Fort, Inc., 2373 W. 700 S., Springville, UT 84663
Distributed by Cedar Fort, Inc., www.cedarfort.com

LIBRARY OF CONGRESS CATALOGING-IN-PUBLICATION DATA

Strain, Elodia Kay, 1979-, author.
 My girlfriend's boyfriend / Elodia Strain.
  p. cm.
 Summary: A romantic comedy in which Jesse, a sassy and intelligent young woman, must choose between two men--one a penniless writer, and the other a successful advertising executive.
 Includes bibliographical references and index.
 ISBN 978-1-59955-905-6 (alk. paper)
 1. Man-woman relationships--Fiction. 2. Dating (Social customs)--Fiction.
I. Title.
 PS3619.T724M9 2011
 813'.6--dc22
                              2011021703

Cover design by Danie Romrell
Cover design © 2011 by Lyle Mortimer
Edited and typeset by Heidi Doxey

Printed in the United States of America

10 9 8 7 6 5 4 3 2 1

Printed on acid-free paper

To my wonderful, beautiful mom, Kathy.
Thank you for being my biggest fan. I'm yours too.

Also by Elodia Strain

The Icing on the Cake
Previously Engaged

before

Girl Meets Boy
by Ethan Reed

INT. SUZIE'S APARTMENT HALLWAY - DAY

ETHAN, a likeable-looking man in his twenties, races down a hallway and stops in front of a door where he starts knocking desperately.

CATIE, a girl about Ethan's age, answers the door.

> CATIE
> Ethan?

> ETHAN
> Catie, where's Suzie?

> CATIE
> She's not here . . .

> ETHAN
> Look, I know she doesn't
> want to see me, but if you'll
> just . . .

                    CATIE
          No, Ethan. She's really not
          here.

                    ETHAN
          Where is she?

Catie looks down, not sure if she should answer.
Ethan sees this.

                    ETHAN (CONT'D)
          Catie . . . I love her.
          Please.

Catie looks at him sympathetically.

                    CATIE
          She loves you, too.

             (pause)

          But she's gone.

Ethan's eyes fill with horror.

                    CATIE (CONT'D)
          She already left for the
          airport.

Ethan bolts. Catie calls after him.

                    CATIE (CONT'D)
          Her flight leaves in 20
          minutes! You're never going to
          make it in time!

   "No!" Barbara, of Barbara Vanderbilt Agency, dropped the
movie script onto her desk with a thud. "Honey, it just feels
formulaic to me. It just doesn't feel . . . real."
   Ethan frowned. "Okay . . ."

Barbara grabbed a fresh strawberry out of a bowl on her desk, her movements dramatic, like someone who'd spent time acting on Broadway. "If you want to break through, you've got to write something with heart. Even a romance has to feel realistic."

Ethan nodded. "That's what I've been trying to do. Draw from real life. Model the character after my own experience."

"That's another problem, hon." Barbara laughed halfheartedly. "You named your main character Ethan? That's not really the kind of reality I'm talking about."

Ethan leaned in, brows knit together.

Barbara shook her blonde curls and bit into the strawberry. "Don't get me wrong—you seem like a very nice kid. But for your leading man you need . . . a leading man. Someone handsome. Confident. Charismatic. In real life, girls end up settling for nice guys like you all the time." She leaned back in her chair. "But they go to the movies to see girls like them falling in love with guys who . . . aren't like you."

"Okay," Ethan said. "So you're telling me you want it to be realistic, but not realistic."

Barbara smiled. "Exactly."

"Okay." Ethan reached for the script. "May I?"

Barbara motioned for him to go ahead.

Ethan took a minute scribbling things out and then slid the script back over to Barbara.

She took a breath and read on.

INT. AIRPORT - DAY

Suzie checks her luggage. As she approaches the security checkpoint, she reaches into her carry-on bag and finds an envelope. She stops and reads the contents of the envelope. Something inside appears to affect her. She runs to the Arrival/ Departure screen and frantically dials a number on her phone.

Cut to ~~Ethan~~ Vladimir. He parks in airport parking and begins ~~running through the airport hallway~~ swiftly moving through the airport in an Italian suit.

Vladimir approaches the Arrival/Departure screen and spots SUZIE. He can't believe it. He approaches her.

                    ~~ETHAN~~ VLADIMIR
          Excuse me.

SUZIE turns around.

                    ~~ETHAN~~ VLADIMIR (CONT.)
          I thought you left.

                    SUZIE
          I thought I would.

They are about to kiss, then . . .

"Okay. Ethan." Barbara looked up slowly. "Your writing is not bad. It's pretty good, actually."

"Thank you," Ethan said, smiling hopefully.

"But it's just not something I can sell."

Ethan looked down, dejected.

Barbara twisted up her fuchsia lips. "I've been watching you come in here for a long time trying to make something happen, and I have to tell you . . . it's just not happening. I'm sorry."

Ethan leaned forward. "There's got to be something else I can do."

"Of course! There's so much you can do! You have your whole future ahead of you. I've heard great things about the Costco Corporation."

"Okay." Ethan stood up from his chair. "Thanks anyway."

Barbara pulled a pained face. "I'm so sorry."

Ethan moved toward the door, and just before reaching for the doorknob, Barbara called out, "Hey, Ethan."

He turned around.

"You know what I'm going to do?"

"What?" Ethan's face was full of hope.

"I'm going to have Allison validate your parking."

"Oh. But I didn't driv—"

Barbara ignored Ethan and picked up the phone, a self-satisfied smile on her face. "Allison. Could you validate this young man's parking?"

Ethan left the office building and found a garbage can on the sidewalk.

He dropped the script right in.

one

Top Ten Rules of Coffee Shop Waitressing

1. Don't ever take a bite out of a muffin you find left on a table. Even if it looks completely untouched. Even if you haven't eaten in 22 hours. Even if you're so hungry you swear the muffin is talking to you, telling you it's okay to eat it. DON'T DO IT.
2. If you see a TV ad for a 20/20 special called "How Dirty Is the Money You Touch Every Day?," skip it.
3. Don't try to boost your tips by attempting bartender-esque tricks like tossing ketchup bottles in the air and trying to catch them behind your back.
4. Same goes for steak knives.
5. Learn to love being called Hey You, Excuse Me, Miss, Honey, Sweetie, Babe, and, every once in a while, when you're having a particularly bad hair day, Sir.
6. Smile.
7. Don't ride the mop like a broomstick when you're cleaning up after closing. (Just because you can't see people outside in the dark, doesn't mean they can't see you.)

8. Ditto playing the broom like an air guitar.
9. Always, always, pawn any group of teenagers off on another waitress. Getting your one-dollar-in-pennies tip out of a smattering of upside-down milk glasses is so not worth it.
10. Be very wary when your boss notifies you of a staff meeting via a note under your car's windshield wiper.

"I thought there was a meeting." I frowned as I looked around the empty break room.

Magda—my boss of eight months, and my Aunt Linda's best friend—looked at me intently. "There is. But it's just for you."

I racked my brain for all the things I'd done wrong since the last meeting.

There was the locking-the-bus-boy-in-the-freezer incident.

And the believing-that-the-college-students-really-needed-empty-whipped-cream-bottles-for-a-school-project incident.

And the spilling-coffee-on-the-mayor-of-Hill-Pointe incident.

My face got hot as Magda handed me a sheet of paper.

I reluctantly looked down and began to read.

Sugar House Coffee: Updated Rules and Regulations (As of March 1, 2011)
Dress Code:
- Skirts should hit at or above the knee, not drag on the floor.
- Thrift store Levi's are no longer allowed—skinny jeans are preferred.
- Tops should not have enough material to make an emergency shelter.

Wait a minute.
I read on, suddenly suspicious.

- Shoes should be comfortable, but not anything you would find on the same website where you would order, say, bags of barley.
- Hair and makeup should not be worn the same way they would be worn for a three-day sit-in.
- Padded bras are encouraged.

I glared at Magda. "Are you kidding me?"

She shrugged innocently as she surveyed my baggy jeans and vintage peasant blouse. "It's for your own safety, hon."

I frowned. "A padded bra is for my safety?"

"When you threw that knife it almost hit—"

"I told you I wasn't going to do that anymore!"

Magda shrugged.

I knew exactly what this was about. The same thing most of my conversations are about these days: My dating life.

Well, my lack of a dating life.

It's weird. If you're not ready to do something like . . . get a dog, no one seems to care.

No one says: Come on, there are lots of nice dogs out there, you might have to go through a couple really awful ones that try to kill you in your sleep, but you'll find a good one eventually.

Or: You can't spend all your Saturday nights in your John Lennon pajamas, watching *Top Chef* and eating Trix right out of the box. You've got to get out there and look for the right one. Maybe try online.

But if you're not ready to date after your heart has been smashed to smithereens—and I mean teeny, tiny, sad, little smithereens—people just can't hold back their ideas/opinions/Dr. Phil-isms.

And sometimes they got really creative.

Customer Service:
- Male customers in the following professions are to

be given free extras (flavor shots, whipped cream, espresso shots, etc.): Medicine, Software Engineering, Dentistry, Software Architecture, Law.

I looked up at Magda. "How did you come up with this list?"

"CNN Money. Top 20 Highest Paying Jobs in America."

I rolled my eyes and kept reading.

• Going the extra mile (even flirting) is a longstanding waitressing tradition—there's no law against touching a handsome, single customer lightly on the shoulder, smiling sweetly, or laughing at a joke every now and then.

I twisted the silver band on my left ring finger and stared at the page.

I guess I shouldn't have been too surprised. After all, I was pretty sure Magda gave me the job at Sugar House solely so she could fix me up.

What makes me think this?

Well, my interview for the job went as follows:

"So, Jesse, tell me about your waitressing experience."

"Well. I don't really have a lot, actually. I've been working at an indie radio station for the last—"

"Great. Moving on. Please fill in the blank. I want to be a waitress here because I like guys with blank color eyes."

I shifted in my seat and looked at Magda for a second, wondering if she'd smile and say she was joking. That she was testing how I operated under pressure or something. But, after a few long seconds, she was still looking at me like she wanted me to answer the question.

So finally I said, "Brown."

The rest of the interview questions were just as strange.

"If a customer were to complain about the food, would you rather date a fireman or an airplane pilot?"

"Sometimes the espresso machine is testy—what's the oldest guy you've ever dated?"

And so on.

So, these new Rules and Regulations were just par for the course, I guess.

I shoved them into my now-outlawed jeans pocket and smiled at Magda. I knew she meant well. "I'll do my best."

"That's all I ask." Magda patted my shoulder. "I'm telling you, Jesse, if I looked like you—with that dark wavy hair, silky smooth skin, and curvy little figure—I'd be running around here dressed like that Lindsay Lohan when she went to court. One day, you'll wake up with bat wings under your arms and stuff growing out of your chin. Take advantage while you can."

I nodded halfheartedly as I moved toward the door. "Got it."

Fake staff meeting now over, I made my way back to the spot behind the counter where I'd been restocking the packets of stevia and cane sugar. As I got back to the job, I let my gaze wander absently to the flowers Magda had let me paint on the shop windows.

And that's when I noticed a guy sitting at a table by the door, scribbling in a notebook. He was seriously cute, with floppy brown hair and a downtown vibe to his jeans and button-down shirt.

I watched him, intrigued by his writing process. He'd jot for a minute. Then he'd scribble out what he jotted. Then he'd take a sip of tea. And then he'd do it all again. Jot. Scribble. Sip . . . Jot. Scribble. Sip.

"Good morning."

The man at the counter startled me. But as soon as I saw his gray hair and goofy medical scrubs—today they had little frogs all over them—a smile came onto my face.

"What's it going to be today?" I asked, my smile widening.

"Just an espresso to go."

"Anything else?"

"Yeah. How about dinner at my place?"

I cocked my head to the side. "I guess I could manage that."

"Good. You've been playing hard to get."

Out of the corner of my eye, I noticed Jot-Scribble-Sip Guy look up for a second.

"Just you then?" the man at the counter asked.

I spun around and began to fill the travel mug he brought in with him. "And David."

"David's always invited. But I just meant you can always bring someone who's not your brother."

I gave him my best warning look as I handed him his drink. "Uncle Logan."

He shrugged. "If I don't ask, how am I supposed to know if there's someone worth asking about?"

"When there is, you'll be the first to know."

Beep. Beep. Beep.

Uncle Logan looked down at his pager, then back up at me.

I lifted my eyebrows. "Hospital?"

"Of course." He held up his cup. "What's the damage?"

I waved him off. "On the house. Doctor discount."

"You're thinking of cops," Logan said. "Doctors pay for their drinks."

"Not according to Magda," I said with a grin. "Now beat it before I change my mind."

Logan waved good-bye, and once he was gone, I looked through the tickets that were starting to pile up next to the register. I quickly noticed one of them belonged to Jot-Scribble-Sip Guy, who, it turned out, was also Orange-Tea Guy.

I added up the total, approached the guy's table, and slapped the ticket down.

And when I say slapped, I mean slapped. My hand hit the table and let out a loud smack that seemed to reverberate through the whole coffee shop.

The guy looked up.

Pretty much everyone did.

"Sorry," I said, massaging my hand. "I didn't mean to startle you."

"Oh no." He smiled a nice, wide smile. "You didn't."

"So," I said, gesturing toward his notebook. "What are you writing?"

"Just . . . some thoughts."

"Like a diary?"

"No," he said, a spark of humor in his eye. "Like a . . . journal."

"Aha." I nodded and moved away to deliver the next ticket in the stack.

But before I got too far, something happened.

Something crazy.

The fear of looking at/talking to/being near a guy that was normally in the pit of my stomach was accompanied by another feeling. A sort of fizzy, brave feeling that told me to look at/talk to/be near this particular guy.

And suddenly, before I knew what was happening, I spun on my heels, moved back to his table, and sat down in the chair across from him.

"So . . . how do I make it?" I asked without preamble.

The guy looked at me, tiny wrinkles forming in his forehead. "Make it?"

I pointed to the notebook. "Into your journal. I mean, how much impact does a girl have to make before you put her in there?"

The guy flipped his pen around in his hand. "Like I said . . . it's just . . . some thoughts. Random really."

"So I have to be more random?"

"Can you be more random?" And there was that smile again.

More random? Of course! As if to prove the point, I did the Hand Jive right there at the table.

I don't know why I do what I do.

But to my utter relief, the guy was still smiling. "Tell you what. I'll name a character after you sometime."

I felt my eyebrows shoot up. "Oh. So you're a real writer. Like, for a living. Would I know anything of yours?"

"Not unless you read the Reed Family Newsletter. Or *The Hill Pointe Free Press*. Which basically have the same circulation."

My eyes got huge. "You do not write for *The Hill Pointe Free Press*! I love that paper!"

"Wait." He leaned toward me. "Seriously?"

"Yes! You guys have the best horoscopes. Mine today was . . ." I looked up, trying to remember the exact wording. "Mars and Venus have aligned in just the right way to make today the worst day of your life. I wouldn't bother leaving the house if I were you. And if you do, don't walk under any power lines or in front of any buses."

The guy laughed. "Ah yes, that's Bethany. Her horoscopes follow her moods."

I shook my head. That explained so much. Like how just yesterday my horoscope said, "Today will be a day of love and luck. You are a magnet for good things. Hug a child. Kiss a kitten. Buy a lottery ticket."

"So what column do you write?" I asked the guy.

He shifted in his seat. "Well. Actually . . . I haven't written in a while because I've been devoting my time to another project. But I was on the public school beat. My name's . . . Ethan Reed."

"Ethan Reed." I scrunched my lips up as I thought. "Wait a minute. Did you write that piece about the ads in the school cafeteria?"

Ethan smiled. But it wasn't a pleased-with-himself smile. More like a surprised smile. "I did."

"I love your writing!"

Ethan looked completely taken aback. "No way. I didn't think anyone read my stuff."

"Well, I do!" I fixed my eyes on him. "So what's this new project you're working on?"

13

Ethan picked up his tea mug. "Well, honestly . . . I'm not working on it anymore."

I could tell there was a story behind that. "When did you stop?"

Ethan looked down at his watch. "Pretty recently."

I met his eye. "You should keep trying. As one of your fans, I think you probably just need to find the right story to tell."

Ethan folded his arms casually. "Okay. Any ideas?"

"Well . . ." I stared at his pen, now on the table. "How about this. A guy walks into a café. He's nice . . . but desperate."

"Desperate?"

"Oh yeah. Total loser." I smiled, surprised by the playfulness in my voice. "Anyway, he's ready to give up all hope. And lo, he meets a girl."

"Did you just say 'and lo'?"

I raised my eyebrows. "Do you want my help?"

"Go on."

"So he meets this girl. The single most amazing creature he's ever laid eyes on." I flashed him a smile. "And she inspires him. Convinces him he can't give up."

"Interesting. What happens next?"

I shrugged. "I don't know. You're the writer."

"So," Ethan said. "Do you think you'd like to—?"

"Miss!" an angry male voice came into my ears. "Miss!"

"Oh!" I hopped up, suddenly realizing he was talking to me. "I'll be back." I grinned over my shoulder as I made my way to the customer and refilled his coffee. After I put the coffee pot back, I ducked behind the counter.

"Who were you talking to?"

"Geez!" I jumped a mile as Magda came up beside me.

"He's got nice eyes," Magda whispered, looking over at Ethan. "Good shoulders."

I bit my lip. "I think he was about to . . . ask me out."

"Well, what do you know?" Magda smiled. "The new rules are already working."

I rubbed my hands together nervously.

"Well, go give him your number," Magda said.

"You think so?"

She shoved an order pad and pen in my face.

Palms sweating, I wrote my name and number on the first ticket in the pad. Then, just for fun, I added a cute-looking smiley face. Or what I intended to be a cute-looking smiley face. But rather than cute, it looked kind of creepy. It said: Call me. I'd like to kill you.

I ripped off the ticket and tried again.

This time, I penned a short poem.

Hey Ethan.
I've been thinkin'.
Here's my number.
Don't make a blunder.
Yeah.

Finally, I gave up the cutesy—and I use that term very loosely—stuff and just wrote my number on the page.

Then, with phone number in hand, I took a deep breath and went back out to Ethan's table. This time I set the ticket down gently and smiled as he picked it up and saw my number.

I winked and walked away.

"But wait," he called to my back. "What's your name?"

I turned around. "Oh, yeah. For the character named after me."

"Well, for that and . . . this." He held up the paper.

Nice. After all that, I forgot my name.

I smiled. "It's Jesse."

Ethan scribbled my name on the paper and put it in his pocket.

And, just like that, I was back in the dating game.

Apparently, the universe got the memo too.

Because not much time passed before something seriously crazy happened.

two

What crazy thing happened?

Well. The coffee shop door opened, and in walked . . . the man of my dreams.

I guess I should explain that a little.

I made the list when I was sixteen.

My Dream Guy
- Looks: Tall, dark hair that's cut short and cute, chin stubble (I love chin stubble), a real smile (not an I'm-too-cool smirk)
- Likes: Alternative and/or classic rock (NO country)
- Has: A job (anywhere other than Hot Dog on a Stick)
- Is: Smart
- Makes me: Laugh (Ren and Stimpy quotes DO NOT make me laugh), feel a little giddy

My crush, Ryan Yardley, had just asked Beth Layton to the Fall Fling, and I was sleeping over at my cousin Laurel's, complaining about the lack of good guys at Hill Pointe North High School.

Laurel ripped two sheets of paper from her biology

notebook and announced that we were going to make Dream Guy lists.

"I read about it in *Seventeen*," she said, through a mouthful of Jelly Bellies. "You make a list of what you want in a guy, and you'll get it."

Mine: See above.

Laurel's: See below.

My Dream Guy

- Looks: Hot
- Likes: Me (and DOES NOT think stupid Jamie Lutz is pretty)
- Has: A cool car (like a Mitsubishi Eclipse)
- Is: A good kisser (If I can describe it using a reptile reference, it's not a good kiss), in a band (*a* band, not *the* band)
- Makes me: Feel special by buying me flowers, candy, jewelry, etc.

A week after we made our lists, Laurel was dating Chad Bowen, who fit all of her criteria. (Except for not thinking Janie Lutz was pretty. Laurel caught the two of them in the back row of the movie theater one night when Chad said he was home with a headache. I'm pretty sure he went home with one for real.)

I, on the other hand, was still dateless and hanging out with the art geeks on weekends, and I quickly forgot about my Dream Guy.

Until now, fifteen years later, when I found myself looking right at him.

Really. See for yourself.

"I'm here to pick up an order."

I stared across the counter at the six-foot-plus, ink-black-haired, five-o-clock-shadowed masterpiece of manhood in front of me. (Tall: Check. Dark hair: Check. Chin stubble: Cha-eck.)

"Name?" I asked.

"Troy Parker. It's to go. And could I also get a cup of your Mexican cinnamon tea?"

"Of course. I'll go get it."

"Thanks." The guy's lips turned up into a smile. It was a cool, casual smile. Like he almost didn't know how good-looking he was. Which, of course, made him even more so. (Smiles for real: Check.)

I swiftly moved toward the kitchen. Once there, I found Magda looking at our handsome customer through the small pass-through.

"Wow," she said. "That is one tasty piece of man meat. If I were a few years younger, I'd be slipping my number into his pocket right now."

I couldn't help but grin as I grabbed Troy's order: A club sandwich and Magda's famous sweet potato fries. When I returned to the counter, I saw my favorite commercial playing on the TV in the corner.

I laughed at a funny part as I set Troy's food on the counter. "My brother and I always die when that commercial comes on. It's so brilliant."

Troy looked over at the TV and nodded his head slightly. "You think so?"

"Don't you?"

"Well, it's just that's . . . my commercial."

I poured some tea into a paper cup. "Your commercial?"

"That's what I do. I write ads." (Job: Check. Smart: Check.)

I bit my lip. "Okay. So, it's only been five minutes, and I've already called you brilliant."

And imagined how much you can bench press.

And thought about how if I worked for Crayola, I'd make a crayon the same color as your eyes, and I'd name it Silky Hot Cocoa.

"I appreciate it," Troy said. "It makes me feel slightly better about being a sell-out. You know, devoting my life to consumerism instead of contributing something artistic to society."

I handed Troy his tea. "Hey, commercials are the art of today's society."

"Huh. My mom says the same thing."

Great. I remind him of his mother. Okay. Must say something not motherly.

"So . . . enjoy your sandwich and fries," I said as I rang up his total. "But don't wash your hands before you eat them. And if you don't finish it all, just throw the rest away. Who cares about the starving kids in China!"

Troy furrowed his brow.

"I mean . . . your total is $13.67."

Troy pulled a credit card out of his wallet. As he did, I noticed a photo of Jimi Hendrix in one of the clear plastic photo sleeves. (Classic Rock: Check.) I handed him the receipt to sign, and after he scribbled on the dotted line, he looked up at me, a smile playing on his lips.

I stared at his mouth, mesmerized. *I could lick your teeth.*

"You could what?"

My eyes shot wide open. I thought I said that to myself!

"Your . . . um . . . your tea." I pointed to the cup he'd set on the counter. "I could click your tea. It's just this thing we do here. Brings good luck."

Troy shrugged. "Okay."

I reached for a coffee stirrer behind the counter and wielded it like a magic wand. I tapped it on the side of Troy's cup three times, and, as if that weren't enough, I added a little chant. "Oh, mighty Mexican cinnamon tea. Please grant this drinker health, happiness, and a long life." I nodded my head and set down the coffee stirrer. "There you go. All set."

Troy was still smiling. "Thank you."

"You're welcome."

He grabbed his bag and held his tea in the air in "cheers" fashion before heading for the door.

Suddenly, I felt a bagel hit the side of my face.

"What the—?"

I turned and saw Magda, a few feet away from me, motioning for me to keep talking to Troy.

I lifted my hands as if to say, "What do you want me to do? He's leaving."

And that's when Troy turned around and came back to the counter.

"You know," he said. "As a general rule, I try not to be one of those guys who ask random girls for their phone numbers. But I have this strange feeling if I don't make an exception in this case, I'm really going to regret it."

I blinked, a giddy feeling rising up inside of me. (Makes me giddy: Check.)

Troy continued. "And then I'll have to come all the way back here. And order this stuff all over again. And find a way to strike up another conversation with you. So . . . if you agreed to give me your phone number now, you'd really be helping me out."

I couldn't help but smile. "You make it sound like an act of charity on my part."

"I don't think there's any other way you could possibly see it."

I laughed. (Makes me laugh: Check.)

And before I knew what was happening, I was grabbing a napkin and scribbling my name and number down.

Troy folded the napkin into fourths and slipped it into his pocket. "Thanks, Jesse. You've done the right thing today." He waved good-bye as he strolled, all manly and hot, out the door.

I watched as he got into a silver BMW parked at a meter right out front and sped away.

And I couldn't help but wonder: Did I do the right thing?

three

I haven't been on a first date in over five years.

Five. Years.

Which means, I haven't been on one since 2006.

Let me take you back to that time: 2006.

Tom Cruise and Katie Holmes celebrated the birth of their little "TomKitten."

The Wii came out—and YouTube was flooded with videos of people throwing those little white remotes into their TVs.

Britney and Kevin called it quits, shocking America to its very core.

Facebook was still just a college campus thing—if you wanted to stalk someone, you had to buy a zoom lens and some night vision goggles.

It was a simpler time.

I stared at my reflection in the mirror, suddenly rethinking everything I was wearing. I ripped off my cargos and purple top and threw them on my bed.

This was all Laurel's fault.

When I called this afternoon and told her Ethan had invited me to dinner at a trendy new place called Lot 21, she sent me text after text that sent my jitters into full-fledged panic.

I'll kill u if u wear anything u bought in a booth

or anything u painted in

or anything made out of men's ties or recycled Coke bottles

or with a political message on it

or with a Beatles lyric/quote/face on it

U CAN wear the Brian Atwood pumps/Hermes scarf/ Marc Jacobs bag I gave u

Oops.

All that stuff was gone.

As an accessories buyer at Saks, Laurel not only gets a great salary, but tons of loot. And when she has too much to hold in her apartment—in one of her many closets or the kitchen cupboards she uses to store shoes and bags instead of food—she passes it on to me. And I may or may not sell most of it on eBay and donate the money to the local animal shelter.

But, just in case Laurel asks, I got robbed and the robber took all the stuff she just mentioned. And my favorite necklace. Just to make it believable.

So now that you've seen Laurel's texts, you know why I was rifling through my closet a few minutes before Ethan was to arrive, seriously freaking out.

Finally, I located a pair of bootcut jeans, a flowy tank top, and an olive jacket. It seemed about right.

I'd just zipped up the jeans when my phone rang. I dug for it in the pile of clothes on my bed and checked the display: Laurel.

"Hey." I turned the phone to speaker and tossed it back on the bed.

"So what are you wearing?"

"Bootcuts. Tank. My olive jacket."

"Eh. I guess that's okay. What about your hair?"

"Wavy. Down. With a little half-up bun thingy."

Laurel sighed. "You should have gone to my hair guy."

I rolled my eyes as I slicked some balm onto my lips.

Laurel has a "guy"—or a "girl"—for everything.

A hand girl.

A scalp guy.

An underarm girl who is apparently a "genius."

"Okay," Laurel said into the phone. "Let's talk about the Save Call."

I searched for my leather wedges in the bottom of my closet. "The what?"

"At exactly 8:12 p.m., I will call you, ready with news of an injury that requires me to be driven to the hospital. I'm thinking a broken ankle." She paused for a second. "Though if it's just sprained, I wouldn't have to miss work . . ."

"You realize you won't actually have an injured ankle, right?"

"Of course." I heard her shift. "So. Anyway. Have your phone in hand at 8:12, so I can save you if the date is bad."

I put some cash into my wallet. "I think I'll be fine."

"That's what my coworker Bethany said when she went out with a guy she just met. She changed her mind when she was sitting through Act Three of the puppet show he put together for her."

"Uh . . ."

"I also wanted to read you some First Date Do's and Don'ts I found in *Miss Magazine.*"

"What?"

"First the Do's. Do touch him on the elbow, bicep, or forearm; draw attention to your eyes and lips; compliment him; maintain good eye contact; and make interesting conversation." Laurel rattled the list off quickly.

"I'm never going to remember all that," I said, my voice kind of panicky.

"Sure you will. Now the Don'ts. Don't floss, pick your teeth, groom yourself, mention any medical conditions, ask overly personal questions, reveal any strange quirks, or cry."

Ding. Dong.

"He's here." I paused for a long second. "Laurel? I'm scared."

"You'll be fine."

"I sure hope so." I hung up the phone and dropped it into my hobo bag.

"Hi. I'm looking for Jesse." The sound of Ethan's voice made my heart beat a little faster.

My brother/roommate/knife salesman responded. "Sure. Come in. I'm David. Her brother."

"Oh. Hey. I'm Ethan."

Scuffle. Slam. Guy silence.

"Jesse!" David called out. "Ethan's here."

"Be right there," I called back.

I took one last look in the mirror, fixing and fluffing.

"You look familiar to me," I heard Ethan say to David. "Have me met?"

Uh-oh.

"I don't think so. It's probably just . . . your eyes."

"No. Wait. You're the guy from the Spry gum commercials!" Ethan said the words like he just solved a math problem.

"Jesse!" David called out loudly.

I grabbed my coat and headed out to the rescue.

When I got to the living room, David had already escaped to his room, and Ethan was looking at a mess of papers on my art desk in the corner: A few of my sketches. The schedule for my art class. A bunch of old horoscopes.

"Hey," I said.

Ethan turned around and smiled broadly. "Wow. You look great."

"Thanks." He was looking pretty good himself, all laid-back and artsy in his button-down, tie, and vintage-looking sweater.

"Are these yours?" Ethan pointed to my sketches: A series I'd made of kids blowing bubbles.

I nodded, feeling my cheeks turn pink. "Yeah."

"They're amazing."

Ethan's words made me feel all warm inside, and I suddenly remembered one of Laurel's Do's.

- Touch him on the elbow, bicep, or forearm.

Before I could lose my nerve, I reached out and touched Ethan's forearm with my fingertip.

But not in a coy, flirty way.

In a weird, poking way.

Ethan looked down at his arm, and I quickly moved my hand away and booked it toward the front door. "Ready to go?"

Ethan nodded and followed behind me.

Please let that be the last lame thing I do tonight.

---·→ ◆ ←·---

It wasn't.

Not even close.

So far, I'd managed to:

Compliment Ethan on his "nice wrists."

Freak him out by staring at him for twelve seconds without blinking because I was trying to "maintain good eye contact."

And, last but not least, talk for a good eight minutes about the oh-so-"interesting" topic of how to properly clean a cappuccino machine.

But, still, somehow, I was having a really nice time as we walked to the restaurant. It was warm outside for March, and the streets were alive with people enjoying their Friday night. It was wonderful to be one of them.

And with such a sweet, cute, funny, guy at my side.

"So," Ethan said as we passed an antique shop. "Your brother's The Gum Guy."

I smiled wryly. "Yeah. But he doesn't really like to talk about it."

"Really?" Ethan shot me an interested look. "Why not?"

I took a breath and got ready to tell the story of how a simple knife salesman from Hill Pointe, PA, became The Gum Guy.

It was the summer of 2010 . . .

Spry chewing gum was running a promotion where people could win prizes in packs of gum. One day, David opened a pack of Spry and saw the words: Grand Prize Winner.

It was kind of shocking, because David is the kind of guy who never wins anything. The guy who finds a coupon in his wallet an hour after it expires. The guy who opens a checking account so he can get the advertised "Free All-Edges Brownie Pan" on the day the bank switches to "Free Deluxe Ballpoint Pen."

Well, it turned out, the "Grand Prize" was a starring role in Spry's new television commercial. Apparently, market research showed gum chewers wanted to see someone "normal" on TV.

I went with David to the commercial taping. The director was this really intense guy in black-framed glasses named Randolph. He seemed happy to see David, his "normal" guy.

Until . . . David got in front the camera.

"Okay, David!" Randolph said. "We're going to start with some shots of you holding the gum, giving us your best gum-commercial smile."

David nodded and held up the gum.

Then he smiled. It was not a gum commercial smile. More of an I-want-to-show-you-all-my-teeth-at-once smile.

Randolph took off his glasses. "Good. But why don't you smile more . . . like a normal person. Like you're smiling at your girlfriend."

David adjusted by opening his mouth a few centimeters, smile still huge.

"That's how you'd smile at your girlfriend?"

David shrugged.

Randolph shot a worried look at Larry, the marketing guy from Spry. "All right. Let's move on to the lines. Can you see the line on the prompter David."

My brother nodded.

"Okay. Go."

(Just so you know, the line was: "Spry gum. Made with xylitol.")

Take 1: "Spry gum. Made with Tylenol—Dang it. Can I start over?"

Take 2: "Spy gum. Made with—Oh wait. I said spy gum. That would be kind of cool. Spy gum. Maybe you guys should look into that."

Take 3: "Spry gum. Made with . . . Xy . . . li . . . How do you say it again? Hey. I like your shirt."

Randolph looked exasperated. He slipped his glasses off and then on again. "Okay, David! Here's what we're going to do. We're going to ad-lib. Why don't you just chew a piece of the gum and tell us how you like it?"

An assistant appeared with a piece of gum and handed it to David. He chewed a few times.

"How is it?" Randolph asked.

"It's gum."

"Can you elaborate?"

"It's . . . definitely gum."

Randolph let out a sigh. "Okay. How about . . . okay. I got it! What would you tell your friends about this gum?"

David thought for a moment then looked at the camera. "It's like mints. But you chew them. And they don't go away."

Randolph took off his glasses, said he was going to take a coffee break, and never came back. Larry took over the direction.

What they were able to make of the ad ran two months later, and David became a bit of a pop culture icon.

There were clips of the commercial on YouTube.

A feature on the news.

And the Gum Guy Halloween costume complete with a cardboard screenshot of David's smile.

"So there you have it," I said to Ethan.

"Wow." Ethan smiled over at me like he had enjoyed not just the story, but also my telling of it.

27

"Yep. David's the best brother a girl could ask for. But not so good at—"

I stopped midsentence when I noticed the huge line outside Lot 21.

Ethan looked suddenly panicked but tried to play it off. We pushed through the crowd, and Ethan went up to the maître d' and talked to him for a moment.

He came back looking at a loss.

"You know what," I said, having a sudden inspiration. "I know a better place."

A few minutes later we were in the Asian grocery store I frequented.

"Jesse," Mr. Choi, the store's owner, instantly recognized me.

"Hi, Mr. Choi."

"We have the stuff you ordered," he said in his heavy accent.

I stared at Mr. Choi for a minute, confused.

And then I remembered: The stuff from the Made in China catalog he always had sitting on the counter. The stuff that seemed just too interesting not to try.

Yes, I'm a catalog/infomercial/in-flight magazine maker's dream. Yes, I have a pair of pajama jeans. Yes, I gave my grandma a set of easy-thread needles for Christmas. Yes, I open my cans with a one-touch can opener.

Problem was, my catalog purchases definitely violated the "Don't let him see your weird quirks" rule.

"I didn't order anything," I said, trying to send Mr. Choi a silent message with my eyes.

"You have a problem with your eyes?" he asked. "We have herbs for that."

"No. I—" I looked at Ethan, trying to think of something, anything to do. But I couldn't think fast enough.

"Here you go." Mr. Choi set my goods on the counter one by one.

The bold, bright wording on the boxes sent a shockwave of humiliation up my spine.

Flashlight Slippers: Walk and See in the Dark!
Slimming Silicone Belt: For Big Thighs and Calves!
Magic Back Stretcher: Bend Over and Feel Better!

I quickly grabbed the products and shoved them into one of the canvas bags hanging from a rack beside the counter. "Thanks, Mr. Choi. I'll pick them up later. We're just here for some dinner."

Mr. Choi smiled and moved toward the little hot-food area in the back of the store. He boxed up some noodles, veggies, and rice for me, and some eggrolls and orange chicken for Ethan.

Two drinks and some Skittles and we were out the door.

"So where are you taking me?" Ethan asked.

I smiled secretively as I made my way down the block and turned the corner.

Finally, we reached our destination.

"Here we are!" I said, throwing my arms in the air, my back facing the surprise locale.

Ethan frowned.

That wasn't what I planned on.

I turned around and narrowed my eyes. City Sanitation Department. What?

I frowned and peered across the street. There I saw the entrance to the baseball field I thought I'd been presenting to Ethan.

With a laugh, I crossed the street and motioned for him to follow. "Come on. You're gonna love it."

When we got to the field's entrance, my plan hit another snag.

It was locked.

I looked around, trying to think on my feet. "Well," I said after a minute. "I guess . . . we can jump the fence."

Ethan looked at me quizzically as I set my food down on the ground.

Okay. You can do this.

I took a deep breath and ran toward the fence. I jumped

up, channeling my inner superhero. When I grabbed onto the chain links, I was sure I was a few feet off the ground. I looked down. I was maybe six inches up. Maybe.

"Hey look," I heard Ethan say. "There's an opening over there."

Oh, thank goodness.

Half an hour later, we were sitting facing each other on the grass in the outfield, our empty food containers on the ground beside us.

It was so quiet out there. Peaceful. I pushed my nerves, and Laurel's First Date Do's and Don'ts, out of my mind and just let myself . . . be.

"I haven't been here in a long time." I took a sip of my lemonade and looked up at the empty stands.

Ethan leaned in toward me. "Are you really sure it's okay for us to be here after hours?"

I smiled, enjoying what I was learning about Ethan. He was vigilant. Considerate.

"After hours is the best time to come."

"Yeah. Until they release the hounds on us."

I grinned. "Hounds?"

Ethan shrugged.

"We're not bothering anyone." I took in a breath, smelling the grass, the ground, the air. "When I was little, my dad used to take me and my brother to games here all the time."

"Are you still close to your dad?"

I looked into Ethan's eyes, a small prickle in my chest. "He died when I was twelve."

Ethan flinched like he'd been hit. "I'm so sorry."

"It's okay. It was a long time ago. But, yeah, we were close."

"What was he like?"

I smiled. Very few people ask me that. And I just loved that Ethan did. "Amazing. He could fix anything: cars, sink faucets, broken appliances. One time, I got this silver remote-control Barbie Corvette for Christmas. I thought it was the coolest thing I'd ever seen. But after two hours of playing with it, my cousin Laurel broke it. I went to Dad and begged him to fix it, and I told Laurel if he couldn't, I'd never talk to her again, and I'd flush my half of our Best Friends necklace down the toilet."

Ethan laughed. "And he fixed it."

"Yep."

Ethan nodded. "I respect that. I work for the management of the apartment building where I live. And I spend a lot of time trying to fix things."

"And how has that gone?"

"Never met a radiator yet that got the best of me. I'm like 12 and 0." Ethan sipped his drink. "What about your mom?"

"Right now she lives in a tech-free commune outside of Seattle. How about your family?"

"Well," Ethan adjusted his legs, "my parents have been happily married for over forty years."

"Wow. That's impressive."

"Yes they are."

"So what's their secret?"

"You got me. They said they fell in love the first night they met." Ethan looked up at the sky and then down at me. "Do you think that's even possible?"

"Um . . . I think I felt that once."

"What happened?"

"Well . . . we dated. We got engaged. We got married." I took in a long breath. "And we got divorced."

"Is that the long version of the story?" Ethan asked, eyebrows raised.

"That's the long and the short of it."

"So what was it?" Ethan's voice was suddenly a little softer. "He just wasn't the right guy?"

"No." I paused, feeling the familiar sting in my chest. "I wasn't the right girl."

Ethan looked at me, like he could tell there was more.

And there was. So much more.

I filled my lungs with the cool, fresh air and lay on my side, my arm propping up my head. "We were married for more than three years. And then . . . we weren't. I tried to make it work."

Ethan mirrored my lying position. "But?"

"But I just . . . wasn't what he wanted." I shook my head. I had not planned on talking about this.

Laurel would kill me if she knew.

Really.

Here are more of the texts she sent me before my date.

I'll kill u if u talk about ur weird obsession with musicals

the crazies in ur art class

ur loser ex-husband

how Jimi Hendrix died too young

how John Lennon died too young

how Kurt Cobain died too young

how Elliott Smith died too young

"Wow," I said, suddenly feeling fear and regret. "How's that for ruining the date?"

Ethan's grin made me feel immediately at ease. "Not even close. I once took out a girl who got back together with her ex-boyfriend through a text message while we were still at dinner. But she didn't tell me until after she ordered a shrimp cocktail, lobster entree, and twenty-dollar dessert that she took two bites of and then covered with salt so she wouldn't eat any more. You're going to have to do a lot better than that."

I smiled, warmed by Ethan's sweetness. I rolled onto my back and stared up at the stars. Ethan followed suit, and my heart sped up as I felt the warmth of him beside me.

"It's funny," I said. "How life doesn't turn out the way you plan. I used to be a planner. I used to have lists. I always thought that by now I'd have my 'Big Dream.' Married. Four kids. House outside the city. Front loading washing machine.

Instead, I live with my brother, and I don't even have a plant."

"You've still got time." Ethan's voice was soft and even. "I bet you'll be a great mom."

The words seemed heavy in the air, and I closed my eyes, my chest rising and falling. "So any first date regrets?" I asked.

"Absolutely not. You?"

"Absolutely not."

After a moment, I felt Ethan's hand graze mine, and I jumped at the touch, sending his drink toppling over. He sat up quickly to pick it up. I could feel him get tense, as if he were regretting his move.

So when he lay back down next to me, I scooted closer to him, so the sides of our bodies were touching.

No regrets whatsoever.

four

I was about to go into a guy's apartment.

And it was really, really weird.

My heart fluttered in my chest as Ethan unlocked the door and I followed him inside.

"So, this is it," I said as I took in the laid-back and homey feel of the hand-me-down couches, loaded bookshelves, and vintage movie posters.

Ethan set his keys on a bookshelf just inside the door. "If by 'it' you mean 'all there is,' then yes, this is definitely 'it.'"

I poked around the shelf. I inspected Ethan's DVD collection—a ton of classics, some indie stuff, and every *Star Wars* film ever made—and then picked up a small, framed photo of him with two blond-headed kids. His smile was almost as huge as theirs. It was quite possibly the cutest thing I'd ever seen.

"My niece and nephew," Ethan said proudly.

My heart turned to marshmallow-y mush. "Aw."

I set the photo down, and picked up another—this one of Ethan and a girl who looked about twelve and who was holding a huge trophy.

"That's me and Maddy Gilbert," he explained. "Her family lives in the same neighborhood as my sister. Maddy won the

citywide middle school science fair with her project: 'Will Retinol or Peptides Work Better on My Mom's Wrinkles?' I wrote
an article about it for *The Hill Pointe Free Press*. Now that's hard-
hitting journalism right there."

"So which one worked better?" I asked.

"Retinol, believe it or not," Ethan said with a nod.

I replaced the picture and picked up a Darth Vader figurine
I noticed perched on the top of the bookshelf.

Ethan quickly grabbed it. "That's just . . . sort of a good luck
thing." He used the edge of his sweater to buff out my finger-
prints.

"I think everything a person owns says something about
who they are," I said.

"What does this say?" Ethan asked.

That you're adorable.

"That you're old school. That's not new. It's an original." I
narrowed my eyes. "I'm thinking . . . Kenner, circa 1977."

Ethan looked at me in shock. "That might be the hottest
thing a girl has ever said to me."

"Don't be too impressed." My mouth turned up in a flirty
smile that surprised me. "I have a brother, remember? I myself
was a My Little Pony girl. My favorite was Firefly. I carried her
everywhere. I washed her mane and tail with Nexxus shampoo
I stole from my mom's bathroom. My cousin Laurel offered me
one Barbie, two Kens, and three scratch-and-sniff sticker books
for Firefly. I turned her down flat."

Ethan set Darth back on the shelf gingerly. "But you weren't
a big enough nerd to keep her into your adult years."

"Oh, I would have." I took in a breath. "But, tragically, Firefly was lost on a family trip when I was seven. I still suspect foul
play."

Ethan moved toward the large couch in the center of the
room. "I'm sure wherever she is, she's very happy."

I followed behind him. "As long as she's a well-adjusted,
adult pony."

Suddenly, I noticed the clock on the wall read 8:12.

Sure enough, seconds later, my phone rang in my bag. I quickly fished it out and checked the Caller ID. It confirmed what I already knew. "Sorry." I shot Ethan an apologetic look. "I should probably get this."

If I didn't, Laurel would keep calling until I did.

"Go ahead." Ethan headed toward the adjoining kitchen. "I have to make our dessert anyway."

"Thanks." I pushed Talk. "Hey."

"Call me Aunt Ida."

"What?"

"So he doesn't get suspicious. Say, 'Hi, Aunt Ida. I haven't heard from you in a while.'"

"Hi, Aunt Ida. I haven't heard from you in a while."

"Good," Laurel said. "So is he smelly? Obnoxious? Boring? Did he go to the bathroom in the restaurant and come back with five rolls of toilet paper and ask you to put them in your bag because, 'Dude, that stuff is expensive'?"

"No."

"No, Aunt Ida," Laurel prompted.

"No." I sighed. "Aunt Ida."

"So everything's okay?" Laurel sounded almost surprised.

"Yep."

"Where are you right now?"

I looked at Ethan in the kitchen. He was slicing some strawberries. "Yep."

"Ohhhh." I could hear the smile in Laurel's voice. "Are you at his place?"

"Uh-huh."

"Nice. Okay. So can he hear you?"

"Sure can, Aunt Ida."

"Perfect! I was going to text you, but this will work better. I found an article called, 'What Makes a Woman Irresistible to a Man.' It wouldn't hurt to mention some of these things while Ethan can hear you."

"Um . . . Thanks for thinking of me, Aunt Ida. But I'm kind of busy. Can I call you tomorrow?"

"No, you can't call me tomorrow, you ungrateful brat. Aren't you appreciative of the five dollars I give you on your birthday every year? And all those times I took you for frozen yogurt!"

Oh, brother.

"Come on," Laurel pressed. "Just a couple things."

I don't know why, but Laurel can talk me into pretty much anything. She's been able to since we were kids.

"Okay, Aunt Ida." I rolled my eyes. "I'm listening."

"Great. Here we go. The first thing in the article is intelligence. So . . . say something intelligent into the phone."

"What?"

"Say something smart."

"Pi over cosine equals hypotenuse."

"Wow!"

So I guess I shouldn't tell her I totally made that up.

"All right. Next on the list is . . . innocence. Say something innocent."

"I've never mugged anyone," I said flatly.

"Good enough."

The sound of Ethan squirting spray whipped cream came into my ears. All I wanted was to get off the phone with Laurel and get back to being with him. "Okay, Aunt Ida," I said. "I gotta go now."

"Fine," Laurel said. "I'll let you go. But if you can, try to let him know you're mysterious, you're not clingy, and you take care of your body."

"Sounds good, Aunt Ida."

"Details tomorrow."

"Of course."

"And I'm going to text you another article I found. 'Top Five Ways to Kiss a Guy to Drive Him Wild.'"

I shook my head.

Like I was going to read that.

And I didn't.

I accidentally skimmed it because I thought it was something else.

"Bye, Aunt Ida."

I hung up the phone and looked up to see Ethan approaching with two plates. On them were Twinkies he'd made into little strawberry shortcakes. He handed me one along with a plastic fork.

"Thanks," I said, grinning at how cute and creative Ethan's "homemade dessert" was.

"So." Ethan sat on the couch next to me. "Is everything okay with Aunt Ida?"

I took a bite of the shortcake. It was actually kind of delicious. "Yeah. She's fine. Just wanted to talk."

"So you don't think she'll call back later to tell you she needs a ride to the hospital? Or . . . to tell you your cousin ran over your dog? Or that Uncle Stu just got arrested and needs you to bail him out?"

I stared at Ethan, and his mouth turned up in a knowing grin.

Busted. "Don't worry. She won't be calling again."

"I take that as a good thing."

"It is. And this." I pointed to the treat with my fork. "Is delicious. I especially like the fresh strawberries. I probably would have just bought those horrible ones in the jar."

"Not much of a cook?" Ethan asked in between bites.

"No. I tried to learn when I was younger but I had . . . a bad experience in a cooking class in high school."

"Really?" Ethan looked intrigued. "What happened?"

I shook my head, lips pressed tightly together. "I'm not telling."

"So did you go to school around here?" Ethan asked.

I licked some whipped cream off my fork. "Hill Pointe North."

Ethan pointed to himself. "Hill Pointe East."

"Well, what do you know? So were you into writing back then?"

"Editor of the school newspaper," he said.

I felt my lips turn into a smile. I could just see him, writing about the food in the cafeteria and the graffiti on the bathroom walls.

"What were you into?" Ethan asked.

"Well, I was in the French club for a while. But then I realized I couldn't speak French. Then I was in the drama club. Until I realized I couldn't act. So . . . I started the Reduce, Reuse, Recycle Club." I lifted my chin in the air, feigning self-impression. "It's still going strong."

Ethan nodded in approval. "So—"

Knock. Knock. Knock.

The knocking on Ethan's front door was loud and frantic and didn't let him finish saying, "So, I've always been really attracted to women who recycle. Where have you been all my life?"

"Ethan!" I heard a woman's voice call through the door.

Suddenly, a bunch of scenarios ran through my mind.

It was his ex-girlfriend. She was still completely obsessed with him, and she was standing on the doorstep with a golden locket Ethan gave her in one hand and a meat cleaver in the other.

It was Ethan's long-lost twin. She'd been searching for him since the day they were separated at birth.

It was his quiet but strange neighbor. She was going to ask Ethan for help with the radiator in her apartment, and then she'd kidnap him and force him to rob banks for her.

Hmm. I may need to stop watching *Lifetime* movies.

Ethan excused himself and swung open the door, and there stood a forty-ish woman in a pair of silky pajamas. "Oh, thank goodness you're here, Ethan!" she said frantically. "Ernesto got stuck in the trash chute again!"

"Mom!" I heard a little voice yell. "It stinks in here! And I think I felt a rat run across my leg!"

"I'm coming, Ernesto!" the woman called back.

Instantly, Ethan sprung into action, grabbing a tool belt from a hook by the door.

"Will you be okay for a little while?" he asked me, an adorably worried look on his face.

"Of course. I'll just poke through all your stuff."

Ethan flashed me an apologetic smile before rushing out and shutting the door behind him.

Suddenly all alone in his quiet apartment, I sat back down on the couch, this time where Ethan had been sitting.

Well, actually, if I'm being totally honest, I used the bathroom first. I'd had to go for a while but didn't know what the first date etiquette was on that, so I'd been doing a lot of leg crossing.

But back to the couch. As I sat down, I noticed something wedged in between the cushion and the arm. It was a huge stack of pages, bound together with a soft binding. I flipped to the first page and saw that it was a movie script.

Curious, I started to read, and was immediately sucked in. I'd never read anything like it. I liked the unusual formatting, the vivid descriptions, and the dialog, which was interesting and witty.

I got completely lost in it.

So lost that when Ethan returned it felt like he'd only been gone for a few minutes. Maybe he had. I'm not exactly sure how long it takes to free a kid from a trash chute.

"Hey there," he said. "I'm really sorry about that."

"So is he okay?" I asked, looking over the back of the couch at Ethan.

He went into the kitchen and washed his hands. "He's fine. Smells horrible, but fine. I just had to unscrew the metal plate and he crawled out."

"Thank goodness he's all right."

Ethan came into the living room, and almost immediately, I noticed all of his natural ease evaporate and his jaw tighten. I quickly realized it was because of the stack of pages on my lap.

"Is this . . . okay?" I asked.

Ethan sat down beside me. "Yeah . . . no. It's fine. It's just . . . I forgot that was there."

I traced the edge of the pages with my finger. "It's really good."

Ethan scratched his head, leaving his hair sticking up in the most adorable way. "No." He looked at me hopefully. "Really?"

"Really. How long have you been writing?"

"Pretty much my whole life."

"Do you have more?"

Ethan shifted uncomfortably. "Some. A few shoe boxes in the closet. And under the bed. And in that little drawer under the oven. What the heck is that for anyway?"

"Who knows?" I laughed and held up the script. "So is it stuff like this?"

Ethan nodded. "Some of it. I also have some short stories. And a couple of ill-advised poems."

"I want to see!"

Ethan frowned. "Oh . . . yeah . . . um . . . I don't really let people . . . read my stuff."

"Might be a problem for a writer."

Ethan leaned back into the couch. "Yeah. I used to think this was what I'd do for a living. That everything else I was doing was just leading up to the point where I broke through with . . . something. But I've discovered it's a lot harder than I thought."

I scooted closer to Ethan. "Maybe you just need more time."

He stared straight ahead, silent. "So what's your thing?" he asked after a minute. "The thing you love to do more than anything else?"

I blinked, my eyes meeting his. "You know, no one has ever asked me that before." I paused for a beat then said, "Art. I love to create. Everything from sketches to watercolors to nerdy things like scrapbooks and cross-stiches. I just love to use my hands to . . . make something pretty out of something plain. In fact, I teach an art class two days a week."

"I like that." Ethan moved his arm, as if he was going to put it around me but stopped and scratched his ear instead.

I lifted his arm and wrapped it around me, making the move for him, and rested my head on his shoulder. And then we just sat like that, completely still and quiet.

And I realized I felt safe and warm for first time in a long time.

five

"And then . . . ?"

I tossed three bags of Whole Foods brand frozen raspberries into my cart. "And then I went home."

Laurel grabbed a pint of Ciao Bella coconut sorbet and dropped it into the basket, on top of my bread. "Boring."

"Actually, it was kind of amazing."

My cousin fixed her eyes on me, obviously surprised by my words.

I was kind of surprised too. I'd been terrified of getting back into the dating game. But Ethan had made things so . . . easy.

Which, unfortunately, made them pretty darn complicated.

"Well," Laurel said. "Now we just need to find his 'Belly Button the Size of an Oreo.'"

I shot my cousin a blank stare. "What?"

"You know. You start to date a guy who seems great, and all of a sudden you learn something about him that changes everything. Need I remind you of my most recent discoveries? Kenny Laughlin: Kissed his mom on the lips. Aaron Bradley: Clipped his toenails with his teeth. Dean Schmidt: Wanted to be a teacher." She closed her eyes and shook her head. "And Jason Grant: Belly button the size of an Oreo. So now we need to find out what Ethan's deal is. Ethan . . ."

"Reed," I filled in.

Laurel pursed her lips. "Ethan Reed: Has fingers for toes."

"You're insane, you know that."

Laurel shrugged.

"I just need to get some Gardenburgers and then we can go." I moved a few feet down the aisle and stopped. "Hey. I think that's the lady who came over to Ethan's last night."

"The one with the kid who got stuck in the trash chute."

"Yeah."

"Hmm . . ." Laurel eyed the woman, who was sifting through the gluten-free bread at the far end of the aisle.

I resumed pushing the cart. "Two times in two days. Crazy."

"So did she see you in there?" Laurel asked after a moment.

"Did who see me in where?"

"Did Garbage Chute Boy's Mother see you in Ethan's apartment?"

"No. I was kind of hidden behind the life-size Storm Trooper cut out."

Laurel eyed me.

"Shut up."

I opened the door to the freezer case that contained the Gardenburgers and tossed two boxes into the cart. "Okay. I'm ready. Let's go check out."

"Or . . ." Laurel put her hand on the cart.

Oh. No.

I knew that "Or . . ."

Many of the most horrifying experiences of my life have started with that "Or . . ."

The time I said: "Guess what, Laurel. I'm going to the salon to get a perm on Friday."

And she said: "Or . . . I could give you a home perm today."

The time I said: "I think I'm going to start plucking my eyebrows."

And she said: "Or . . . my mom has this Nair stuff in her shower that will take the hair right off."

The time I said: "I think I'm going to give Ben Lutz a note that says I like him."

And she said: "Or . . . you could write him a song and ask the school secretary to let you sing it during the morning announcements."

"Or what, Laurel?" I asked, not wanting to know the answer.

"I have an idea."

"Wha—?"

Before I could finish, Laurel pushed my cart to the side, grabbed my arm, and dragged me in the direction of the woman.

"Just go with me on this," she whispered. "You'll be glad you did."

And that's all it took. I really don't know how she does it.

I followed behind as Laurel sidled up to the woman. "Excuse me," she said cheerily.

The woman set two loaves of bread in her cart. "Yes?"

"My name is Laverne." Laurel pointed to me. "And this is Shirley."

Oh, boy.

"We're doing a survey," Laurel continued. "And we were wondering if we could ask you a few questions."

"What's the survey about?"

"Apartment managers."

What? I narrowed my eyes at Laurel.

"I guess," the woman said with a shrug. "I used to work in telemarketing, so I know what it's like to—"

"That's nice," Laurel cut her off. "So you're giving your consent to participate?"

"Sure."

"And you live in an apartment?"

"Yes."

"Great," Laurel said. "And what's your first name?"

"Rosa."

"Okay, Rosa. Here we go." Laurel retrieved a notebook from her Louis Vuitton bag and opened to a page that I could see was a list of items she needed from the drugstore. "A recent study done by . . . the National Institute for Studies International shows that nine out of every eight people don't know simple things about their apartment managers."

"Hmm," Rosa hummed.

"It's a shame," Laurel said. "A sad commentary on how we just don't care about one another anymore."

Rosa looked at me.

I nodded solemnly for effect.

Laurel straightened her back, her chin-length blonde bob swishing as she did. "I am going to ask you a series of simple questions about your apartment manager. Please answer to the best of your abilities. If you don't know, simply say you don't know."

Rosa nodded. "Okay."

I've gotta admit, I was more than a little impressed with Laurel's improvisation. And more than a little interested in Rosa's answers.

"Is your apartment manager male or female?"

"Male."

"Excellent." Laurel pretended to write the answer in her notebook. She instead added razors to her list. "Does your apartment complex have a pool?"

"Yes."

"Have you ever seen the manager swim in that pool?"

"Yes."

"And when you saw him swim, did you see his belly button?"

"What?"

"Did you see his belly button?" Laurel repeated slowly, like it was the words Rosa was having trouble with.

"These are very . . . odd questions." Rosa moved like she was going to look at the notebook.

Laurel hugged it to her chest. "Yes, well, science is an odd thing. These questions are specifically designed by expert study designers. So. Would you say his belly button was . . ." She moved the notebook away from her chest and looked down at it. " . . . Large, medium, or small?"

Rosa cleared her throat awkwardly. "Small."

"Great. And did you see his back?"

"His . . . ?"

"How hairy was it?" Laurel pulled a face. "Are we talking carpet?"

Rosa's frown deepened. "Actually . . . these questions are making me a little uncomfortable. I'm pretty sure I have the option to opt out at any time."

"Sure," Laurel said. "But do you want to opt out? That's how we as a society have gotten to this point. We just 'opt out' of knowing each other."

Rosa held onto the handle of her cart. "Okay . . ."

"Since you're clearly uncomfortable," Laurel said. "We'll move on from the physical questions and get to the social ones."

"Thanks," Rosa said.

"How close do you live to your apartment manager?" Laurel asked.

"Three doors down."

"Great."

"Is his mother over at his apartment a lot?"

Rosa shook her head. "Not that I've seen."

"Are people dressed in costumes related to any science fiction books and/or television shows over a lot?"

"No."

"Has he ever mentioned belonging to any of the following: An a cappella singing group, a medieval fighting troupe, any group ending with the word 'anonymous'?"

"Not that I can recall."

"Have you ever seen him dressed in any of the following: Cut-off shorts, socks with sandals, penny loafers?"

"Nope."

"Great. Well, I've asked you all my questions. Shirley." Laurel elbowed me and handed me the notebook.

I stared at it for a long second, feeling awful for lying to this poor lady. But . . . there were a few things I wanted to know.

"Okay, Rosa," I said finally. "Would you say your apartment manager dates to have fun, to find love, or to settle down?"

Rosa thought for a minute. "To find love. And probably to settle down."

Her answer hit a nerve inside of me. I cleared my throat and asked another question. "And would you say he dates a lot, a little, or somewhere in between."

"A little," Rosa said quickly. "I don't see him with many girls. He seems to be very cautious, and very selective."

"So, uh, how many girls have you seen him with in the past week: One, two, more than two?"

"One. At his apartment last night. I came over for something, and I saw her."

"Really?" I asked with a smile. "And could you describe her for me?"

Rosa shrugged. "She definitely didn't look like anything special."

My smile evaporated. She couldn't have seen more than the top of my head, and maybe my foot. What could she tell from that?

"But you didn't talk to the girl, did you?"

"No."

"So for all you know, she might be smart, caring, and creative. She might love her family. She might be able to play Home on the Range on the harmonica while standing on her head?"

"Maybe. But I doubt it."

"Do you, Rosa?" I asked, eyes narrowed. "Do you doubt it?"

Rosa frowned at me. "Yes. When I got to his apartment, he couldn't get out of there fast enough."

Because he was trying to free Ernesto! And, come on, whose kid gets stuck in a trash chute?

"I'm just saying." Rosa shrugged. "I don't think it's going to last. I think he's going to go for Maggie."

"Maggie?" The word came out all froggy. I cleared my throat. "Could you please, for the survey, tell me about this Maggie? Does she have a big head? Dramatically different-sized ears?"

Rosa leaned against her cart. "I've never seen her or anything. But I go to my friend Kim's house a lot, and she lives next door to the manager. A few weeks ago, he started talking to his sister about a girl named Maggie. We don't go out of our way to listen or anything, but the walls are pretty thin. Anyway, he's talked about how smart she is, how young she is, how cute she is, and how she calls and texts him all the time."

"I see."

"But that's all I know. Now. I really have to go." Rosa looked perturbed as she pushed her cart away and resumed her gluten-free shopping.

Laurel grinned and linked her arm through mine as we dashed back to the cart, which luckily was still where we'd left it. "I'd say that went pretty well."

I glared at her as I swiftly pushed the cart toward the checkout. "You would?"

"Absolutely. You have the answers to a whole bunch of questions, don't you?"

"Um . . . yeah . . . I guess."

six

Dinner? Rue 8 French Cuisine. 7:00.

I got that text from Troy at ten minutes to six. There was something about the spontaneity of it that I liked.

Flying by the seat of my pants isn't something I've ever been really good at, but lately I've been trying to live more freely. It's a lot easier than making lists and plans that just get messed up anyway.

I didn't give myself time to think before responding.

Sounds good.

So now, here I was, sitting across from Troy at Rue 8, an insanely chic French restaurant, panicking as I read over the menu.

Why? Because it was entirely in French.

Which I may have led Troy and the waiter to believe I was fluent in.

I'm sorry, but there was just something about the way the waiter asked me in his uber-thick accent, "Do you need help with the menu, mademoiselle?" that made me say, "No, I'm fine. I spent much of my childhood frolicking through the streets of Paris."

Now I was staring at the swirly words on the page, willing one, just one, of them to make sense.

But no such luck.

It's not that I'm a picky eater. (Trust me, as a non-cook, I can't afford to be. I had Wheat Thins with peanut butter and salsa for lunch today.) It's just that I don't eat meat. And at about fifty bucks a plate, I didn't want to order something I couldn't eat.

Wait a sec. I just thought of something. Maybe you could help me.

Yes! That's perfect! I'll just read a few of the menu items to you and you can tell me if you know what any of them are. Okay. Ready?

Chateaubriand.

Cassoulet.

Pate de foie.

Canard a la Orange.

La frisée.

Do you have any idea what those things are?

If you do you write it in here:

_____.

Dang it. The waiter just came back. Thanks anyway.

"You ready to order, mademoiselle?"

"Almost," I said, scanning the menu like I read French every day. "I'm just deciding between two dishes."

"Wow." Troy said, sounding impressed. "I had no idea you spoke French."

"*Oui. Je m'appelle stylo.*" I twisted my hand in the air with what I thought was a French flourish.

And, by the way, *Je m'appelle stylo* = My name is pen.

The waiter smiled smugly as I ordered what I hoped was a salad.

Either that or a duck liver.

Troy ordered next, his French sounding completely flawless. But what do I know? My name is pen.

"So I take it you come here a lot," I said as the waiter left with our orders.

"Some," Troy responded. "I work just down the street."

"Really?" I raised my eyebrows. "So you take a lot of your dates here then."

Troy flashed me that smile of his. The one that made a girl feel lucky to be with him. "Only the ones I want to impress."

"Well, I'm not really impressed by a fancy meal." It was kind of a lie. I was feeling so special, so giddy, sitting across from him in the luxurious banquette, the candlelight flickering.

"Looks like I'll have to work harder to impress you then," Troy said.

"Okay." I nodded. "What've you got?"

"I can spell the word Connecticut."

I folded my arms across my chest expectantly.

Troy laughed, a flash of mischief in his eyes. "Okay. You got me."

"I'll let it slide." I took a sip of my Perrier. "So how long have you been coming here?"

"Since we started the agency. So I guess . . . just over four years."

"Since *we* started the agency?"

"My business partner and I."

There was something about the way he said "business partner" that told me there was a story there. An interesting one. I was about to ask him about it when the waiter returned with a loaf of the most amazing smelling bread.

"So what do you do when you're not working?" I asked Troy as I sawed off a piece with my knife.

"I play a lot of golf. And I like to travel. Especially to places where there's good diving."

I chewed the warm bread, pretty much in heaven. When you're a vegetarian, bread is pretty important to you. And this bread was becoming very important to me. "You know,"

I dabbed the corners of my mouth with my napkin, "I love to travel. But it seems like I never really go anywhere."

"Not since your childhood in Paris?" Troy's mouth twitched slightly, and I knew he knew.

"Yeah," I said with a grin. "I miss those days."

"So where do you want to go?"

"I have a top four," I said instantly.

Troy motioned for me to continue.

"The Alps. Vail. Tahoe. Park City."

"I'm noticing a trend here," Troy said.

"Yeah. I'm kind of obsessed with snow. Mittens. Sweaters. Cocoa. Sitting in front of the fireplace playing Scrabble. I love it all."

"I've been to the last three but not the Alps," Troy said.

"Was Vail amazing?" I asked. "I've heard the views are just spectacular."

Troy met my eyes. "Nothing compared to the one I'm looking at."

The waiter returned holding our plates and set them down in front of us. I looked down at mine and instantly relaxed.

I'm happy to report: It was a salad.

---→ ◆ ←---

The night was cool and clear.

Troy offered me his jacket, and as I held it around me, I pretended to have a sniffle, so I could inhale its scent: Clean, masculine, expensive.

As we walked, we talked about Troy's love of scuba diving, and the time I let Laurel talk me into fire walking.

"What are your top three favorite movies of all time?" Troy asked as we passed a group of teens on the sidewalk.

"*White Christmas*, *Yellow Submarine*, and *Pride and Prejudice*."

"Which one?" Troy asked, a glint in his eye. "Don't they remake that movie once a year, every year."

"Hey. Mr. Darcy expressing his undying devotion? You can't see that too many times. But . . . I have to admit, the one with Colin Firth is a cut above the others. What are your three favorites?"

"*The Sting, Rocky*, and, of course, *Die Hard*."

I nodded and noticed we were passing one of my favorite buildings in the city.

"I love this place," I said, looking up at the gorgeous brick. "I have a book on Pennsylvania architecture and the guy who designed this building, Raymond Anderson, went to school with Vincent Kling, you know the Philadelphia Love Park guy."

"And the view from the top floor is amazing," Troy said.

"I wouldn't know. I pass it all the time on my way to my art class, but I've never actually been inside."

"Let's go then." Troy grabbed onto my hand and moved toward the building's entrance.

I frowned. "I'm sure it's been closed for hours."

Troy pulled the handle of the glass entrance door. "Yeah. You're right. But . . ." He reached into his pocket and retrieved a key card. "I wonder if this would work."

And just like that, we were on the top floor of the building, walking through a door marked Parker/Kline Creative.

"Wow." I took in the view through the windows that made up one wall of the open-concept office. "This is amazing."

"We like it."

I tore my eyes away from the sparkling city and noted the modern, minimalistic design of the space. "Which one is yours?" I asked, pointing to the cubicles.

Troy walked toward a glass-surrounded office in the corner. *Ah. So this one is yours.*

I looked around, eyes wide. The space was huge, with grand windows, shelves filled with books by people with names like Ogilvy and Deutsch, and home-y touches like a mini-fridge, sitting area, and indoor putting green.

I sat on the arm of the couch in the sitting area and continued to look around in awe.

"So this is the place you call home during the day."

"And some nights," Troy said with a nod. "I spend so much time here, I figured I may as well make it as comfortable as possible."

"It's really . . . big."

Troy smiled. "Yeah. Obviously I'm overcompensating for something. But I'd prefer not to say what."

I shook my head playfully, and my eyes suddenly landed on a bunch of framed magazine articles on the wall.

I got up to inspect them.

There was one that featured a photo of Troy with a few members of the City Council. One with a picture of him wielding a pair of giant scissors at a ribbon-cutting ceremony. And one with a huge, full-page shot of him dressed in a tux, with a lovely redhead in a slinky blue dress standing beside him.

Troy came up behind me as I read the caption below the photo: Troy Parker and Vivian Kline at the Advertising Hall of Fame Induction Ceremony and Gala in New York City.

Kline? Why did that name sound so familiar? I scrunched my forehead up in confusion. But I just couldn't place the name.

I moved closer to the article, pretending to read.

But what I was really doing was studying Vivian's body language.

I probably shouldn't admit this, but you know those articles in the tabloids where the writer takes a photo of someone like David and Victoria and writes a blurb about what their body language says? Well. I read those. All the time.

And let me tell you, as I looked at the photo, I was pretty much positive that had it appeared in one of those magazines, the caption would read: Vivian's hand is tight around Troy's arm, and her head is tilted toward his. Her smile is definitely not professional. Nor is her dress. She clearly wants him.

I opened my mouth to ask Troy who Vivian Kline was, but stopped for some reason and instead feigned a yawn.

Troy looked at his watch. "Man, I didn't realize how late it was. I guess we should get you home."

Darn you, fake yawn! Darn you, Vivian Kline!

"Yeah," I said. "I do have a lot of stuff to do tomorrow for my art class."

Troy shut out all the lights, and we left the office and made our way back out to the street.

"Favorite ice cream flavor?" Troy asked as we resumed walking.

"Mint chocolate chip. So who's the girl in the picture?"

"What?" Troy furrowed his brow. "What picture?"

Okay. Cover. Quickly. "Um . . . *Pirates of the Caribbean*."

"Uh." Troy looked confused. "You're asking who the girl in *Pirates of the Caribbean* is?"

"Yeah. What else would I be asking?"

Troy navigated around a crack in the sidewalk. "The main girl's name is Keira Night . . . something."

"Oh yeah. Keira Knightley. Thanks. That was going to bug me."

We exchanged a few more favorites, and before I knew it, we'd arrived at my apartment building. Troy walked me to my doorstep.

"Well . . . ," he said, his voice low. "I had a great time."

"I don't blame you," I said with a coy smile.

"Wow." Troy leaned against the doorjamb. "Narcissism is hot."

I mirrored his position. "So is sarcasm."

"Well, you can work on that next time," Troy said.

"So you're assuming there's going to be a next time?"

Troy moved close to me, his expression softening. "I hope so."

I blinked, wordlessly looking into his eyes.

56

"So this art class." Troy moved even closer to me. "Can you have visitors?"

I could hardly breathe. "Maybe."

"Well, maybe you'll have one."

seven

I'm going to confess something to you.

And I hope you understand.

In the months after I went from being the girl who had shiny, beautiful life plans to the girl who stopped brushing her hair and started eating Go-Gurt for every meal, I did something I never thought I'd do.

I read . . . self-help books.

I know, I know.

But I just couldn't help it.

I'd wander into Barnes & Noble, dressed in a ratty paint-spattered T-shirt, my hair in a messy braid, looking to make myself feel better with a big cup of hot cocoa and the horoscopes in *OK! Magazine*, and I'd find myself sitting on the floor, among the relationship books.

I read all kinds.

The ones about revenge: *Destroy Him Like He Destroyed You!*

The ones about reconciliation: *Get Him Back by Getting Hot!*

The ones about rebuilding: *He's Gone. Move On!*

But the books that seemed to help me the most were the ones that told me to focus on something other than myself.

There was one written by a lawyer who dealt with his

divorce and job loss by writing a thank-you note every day for a year.

One about a woman whose husband left her via a text, and she responded by buying an RV and volunteering at a women's shelter in every state in the Continental U.S.

And then, on a rainy Saturday, there was one that really struck a chord with me. The book started out with a list of ways to focus outward rather than inward.

- Play with a child
- Read to someone in the hospital
- Serve food at a homeless shelter
- Knit a blanket for a preemie
- Walk a shelter dog

It was the sixth suggestion on the list that really got me:

- Teach someone to do something you love

I stared at the words, my mind spinning. I'd been turning to art so much lately, and teaching it to someone else seemed like the perfect thing to do.

So I opened my computer and started a search. After a little looking, I found an ad that caught my eye.

Wanted: Art Teacher
The Hill Pointe City Center is looking for a qualified art teacher.
Requirements: BA in art or equivalent.
Fax resume to: Darla Knox, darlak@cityarts.web.

I almost skipped over the posting because I don't have a BA in art—I have a BA in International Studies. But something inside made me email my resume, and two days later I got a call from Darla.

"I noticed you don't have an art degree," she said after we'd talked for a minute.

"No. I don't."

Darla was silent for a beat. "Why don't you come by the center tomorrow morning at nine anyway? And bring your portfolio. I have a good feeling about you."

My mouth dropped open in shock. "Thank you! Thank you so much!"

I hung up, determined to convince Darla that I was a true artist, capable of teaching others.

So, the next morning, I dressed in all black (I even threw on a black beret for good measure) and marched into Darla's office with my portfolio—which, let's be honest, was a black binder filled with the post-heartbreak paintings I'd been churning out and everything decent I could find in my high school art folder—under my arm.

Darla took a long time looking over the stuff from my recent "dark period" and said, "So. Who is he?"

"Excuse me?" I asked.

"The man who broke your heart."

"Um . . ."

Darla reached out and took hold of my hand. "Men are the enemy. One minute you're having a nice time in Hawaii, and the next he's telling you he just doesn't know who he is anymore."

I blinked. "Uh . . ."

"And then three months later you're driving down Fifth Street and you see him in a purple Volkswagen Beetle, sporting a silk shirt and a mustache."

More blinking.

"I knew there was something about you," Darla said. "This job is just what you need. Get him out of your system."

Next thing I knew, I had a second job. And for the past five months, I've been teaching art every Tuesday and Thursday night. I've loved every minute. And my lack of technical training hasn't really proven to be a problem.

Until now.

"You must be Jesse."

Brow furrowed, I unslung my bag from across my body, and stared at the serious-looking blonde standing in front of me. "Yeah . . ."

"My name is Ann Walsh. I'm here to observe your class for the day."

What?

I looked out at my group of six students, who were perched on their stools in the open loft space, watching us with interest. "Okay . . ."

Ann removed an iPad from her leather satchel. "Since this is your second term here, I've been asked to observe your class to see how things are going. To make sure you're teaching to Hill Pointe City Center standards."

Oh. No.

"Don't worry," Ann said with a forced smile. "It's mostly just a formality. Simply pretend I'm not here and proceed as you would normally." She smoothed her pencil skirt and took a seat in the corner of the loft.

My heart banged against my ribs. How was I supposed to know if I was teaching to Hill Pointe City Center standards? I could feel sweat forming on my brow, and all I could think about was how she'd discover me. How she'd figure out that I was an imposter.

"Um . . ." I looked out at the class. "Hello, everyone."

The students muttered hellos.

"We have a very educational, mind-expanding class planned for today." I glanced over at Ann. "Let's begin by sharing the drawings we worked on over the weekend."

Normally when we share our work, we just go around the room and everyone makes comments. Mostly "good job" and "that's nice" type comments. But as I looked over at Ann and the iPad on her lap, I had a feeling that wasn't going to cut it today.

Suddenly, I had an idea.

"And as we show our drawings," I said quickly, "I want you

to really talk about what they mean to you, how they make you feel."

The class looked confused.

"Art is about more than what's on the page." I made a fist and held it in front of my heart dramatically. "It's about what's inside of us when we look at what's on the page."

Ann typed something.

"Why don't we start with you, Bill?" I said nervously.

Bill is in his late-forties and is taking the class with his wife, Terry, to spice up their life, and hopefully help them stop bickering.

Bill looked at Ann and then at me.

"Go ahead," I said in my most supportive, art teacher-y voice.

Bill cleared his throat and held up a sketch of a car. "I sketched the Corvette I'm restoring."

"And what does the Corvette mean to you?" I asked.

Bill looked at me, brow furrowed.

"Take your time," I said.

Bill frowned and cleared his throat again.

"Oh, for crying out loud!" Terry huffed. "You can't even answer a simple question."

"I'm doing my best," Bill said softly.

"That's always your excuse isn't it?" Terry asked. "Dr. Cannon was right—you need to set higher standards for yourself."

Bill's face started to get red. "Dr. Cannon also said you should stop berating."

Terry rolled her eyes. "Dr. Cannon's an idiot."

"Yes!" I gestured wildly. "Now we're really getting into it!"

The class looked at me like I was crazy, and Ann typed some more.

I shifted my feet. "Okay. Let's move on. Eldon, what did you draw?"

I looked over at Eldon, a seventy-five-year-old retired attorney. He's the best artist in the class, in my opinion. His favorite thing to do is discuss his many conspiracy theories.

Eldon frowned. "I drew a barcode."

I looked at the sketch. It was actually pretty cool. "And why did you draw a barcode?"

"Because I want everyone to know that they're a way for the government to track us." Eldon made eye contact with each member of the class. "They're watching you."

"Thanks, Eldon," I said. "How about you, Gladys?"

I nodded my head toward Gladys, the fiftyish woman who I'm pretty sure signed up for the class simply so she could have someone to complain to about her many physical ailments.

"I forgot we had an assignment," she said.

I snuck a glance at Ann, who was sitting, legs crossed, waiting for my response.

How would a qualified art teacher respond?

"That's okay," I said. "Art is not always on a timetable. But I'll be waiting to see your work next time."

Gladys nodded. "Sorry. I've been forgetting things a lot lately. I'm thinking it's either my thyroid, lead poisoning, or early-onset Alzheimer's."

"It's the fluoride they put in our water," Eldon said. "They do it so they can control us."

I caught a glimpse of Ann's disapproving face and quickly pointed to Jerome, the cute guitar player who signed up for the class when he found out his ex-girlfriend, Jana, was taking it.

At first it seemed stalkerish to me, but he's totally harmless—I think.

"Jerome," I said. "You're up."

"I sketched Jana." Jerome looked over at his ex and revealed a sketch of her that was actually kind of scary.

"Oh my gosh—" Jana gasped. "Come on, Jerome! How long are you going to act like this?"

"Until you realize we're meant to be together."

Jenna brushed her black bangs out of her eyes. "So never then."

Jerome shrugged. "I wouldn't be so sure."

"It's never gonna happen!" Jana shouted.

"All right!" I pumped my fist in the air. "This is what art is all about! Passion! Lust!"

"And crazy people," Jana said under her breath.

"What did you draw?" I asked her.

"My new boyfriend." Jana smiled her pretty smile as she revealed her sketch of a guy in a business suit. "He's a realtor," she said proudly.

"Now I need to draw my bleeding heart . . ." Jerome flipped to a new page in his sketchbook and started to scribble. " . . . In your hand."

"Jerome drew Jana, and they aren't even together anymore," Terry grumbled to her husband. "Would you ever draw me?"

Bill leaned toward her. "Of course I—"

"Oh, no you wouldn't, you passionless bum."

"Would you like to share your drawing Terry?" I asked, heading off the fight.

"No." She crossed her arms in front of her.

I cleared my throat. "Okay, then. Good job, class. We really got into things. And now that we've discussed our work . . ." I looked at the clock. We had thirty minutes to go. Usually, we'd just do some free drawing or painting and talk about the latest celebrity scandal. But again, that wasn't going to cut it. " . . . It's time for art vocabulary."

My students stared at me, their faces blank.

"Turn to the back page of your sketchbooks," I prompted. "And we'll pick up where we left off."

They all knew we hadn't left off anywhere. But, to my relief, they went along with the charade.

"All right." I sat down on my stool. "We left off on the letter E. So the next word is . . . Eraser. Eraser: An implement used to undo things that . . . look like crap."

The class scribbled in their notebooks.

"Fine art," I continued. "Art . . . of the highest caliber."

Ann frowned.

"Gallery." I held my head up high like I knew what I was doing. "A place . . . where art is."

The class jotted down my words and then stared at me expectantly. I was beginning to think I should have been giving them art vocabulary this whole time.

"Next we have . . . Hue." Wow. I was kind of proud I came up with that. "The way a color looks. Visually. When you look at it."

Ann typed feverishly on her iPad.

"Impressionism!" I shouted. "A type of art consisting of a bunch of splotches that . . . look pretty good together."

"What?" Jerome said. "What was that last part?"

"Check with the person next to you if you have questions."

Jerome whispered to Eldon for a second.

I caught a glimpse of the clock and saw that we had burned through just enough time that we could probably finish with free drawing, and it wouldn't reflect badly on me. Thank goodness. I crossed my arms and leaned back on the stool. "That's it for vocab for the day," I said. "Your assignment for next time is to take photos to use as inspiration for the paintings we're starting. For the remainder of today, you can think about what you might want to photograph, or you can do free drawing or painting. Good arting today!"

Good arting?

The class chattered and worked until it was time to go. I waved good-bye as they all left.

"Well," Ann said, coming up to me. "An interesting class."

An interesting class? I knew what that meant. It's like when people say, "Oh, what a unique-looking baby."

"I think I should warn you that the center is thinking of discontinuing this class," she said.

My mouth shot open. "What?"

Ann shrugged. "Enrollment is down. It's just not bringing

in enough money. This class has a thirty-person capacity and you have six."

"Maybe we just need to advertise more." My voice was panicky. "Or—"

"It won't make much of a difference. People can get online and YouTube an art class. We need to make room for our classes that are bringing people in. Piloxing. Krankinning. Scrogging."

I have no idea what any of those things are.

"Nothing will happen until the end of this term," Ann said. "I just felt like . . . I ought to give you a heads up."

"So you came in today to . . ."

"See if the class is worth saving." Ann frowned. "And I'm not sure it is."

I held out my hands. "I can make it more modern. I can—"

"It's not you; it's the economy."

Ah yes, the 2011 version of "It's not you; it's me."

Ann pulled a sympathetic face and patted me on the elbow before walking out.

I let out a long breath and looked around the empty loft. It had been a sanctuary for me, this class. And I knew it had been one for many of the students. I think even Bill and Terry were getting something out of it.

There had to be something I could do.

Buzz. Buzz.

My phone vibrated in my bag, and I quickly moved across the wood floor to grab it. My frown changed to a smile the second I saw the Caller ID: Ethan.

"Hey," I said into the phone, smile widening.

"Hey back." Ethan's voice sent a nice little wave up my spine. I closed my eyes and pictured him on the other end of the line.

"So," he said. "I just scored exclusive tickets to the biggest event in the city tomorrow night. You in?"

I shimmied my shoulders in glee. This was just what I needed. "Absolutely."

eight

When you hear the words: "Biggest event in the city," what comes to mind?

A play?

A concert?

An art exhibition?

Do you think: Middle School Spring Carnival?

Yeah. Me neither.

But as Ethan pulled his beat-up Jetta into the packed school parking lot, I couldn't help but smile. The entire soccer field had been transformed into a fair—complete with rides, booths, and carts of food.

Ethan grinned as he hopped out of the car and opened my door. "Are you ready for the best night of your life?"

I lifted my eyebrows. "I sure am."

Ethan grabbed my hand and led me to the carnival's entrance booth. He pulled a tag out of his pocket that said, "Press."

The woman in the booth stamped his hand and gave him a roll of complimentary tickets. Then she looked at me. "One adult?"

"She's with me," Ethan said, feigning self-importance. It was so adorable.

I shot him an impressed look as the woman stamped my hand.

And then we were in.

I felt a childlike excitement bubble up inside as I took in the bright lights, the fun carnival games, and the scent of funnel cake and popcorn.

"So," I said as we walked past a ring-toss booth, "I take it you're covering this event."

"That's right."

"So where do we start?"

"I've been told I should start with the miniature golf," Ethan said. "It's supposed to be the best thing here."

"Sounds good to me."

We walked to the back of the field, where a nine-hole miniature golf course had been set up. We stopped at the table at the entrance.

A kid in a knit cap handed us two putters and two balls in exchange for six tickets each. "Good luck," he said, sounding bored. "And thank you for helping support Pinewood Middle School's new . . . whatever."

Ethan raised his putter in the air. "Thanks, man."

We made our way to Hole 1, which was made to look like an Egyptian pyramid, and I gazed around, loving everything about what we were doing. "I can't remember the last time I did this."

"Even more reason to do it."

"I have to admit, I'm not much of a golfer."

"That's too bad." Ethan rested his putter on his shoulder. "Because I . . . am awesome."

"Okay." I shot him a coy look of challenge. "Let's see what you've got."

Ethan put his ball on the ground and lined up his shot. He hit the ball, and it flew wildly off in the completely wrong direction. I laughed as he moved to try again.

The next eight holes were a mix of awful golfing and painful laughing. My stomach was sore by the time we got to the mini waterfall at Hole 9.

"So what's next, newspaper guy?" I asked after I fished my ball out of the waterfall and declared that I was done.

"Now we find the Palm Reading booth. Maddy, the girl from the science fair picture you saw, should be working in it."

"Okay." I was practically skipping. "Let's go."

We navigated through the crowd for a few minutes and soon found a white tent marked, "Palm Reading."

Ethan handed our tickets to the girl outside the tent, and she stood and opened the flap for us. "Welcome. Your future is within."

"Thank you," we said in unison as we ducked inside.

"Ethan!" Maddy—who I barely recognized in her huge hoop earrings, white peasant top, bright skirt, and gold false-eyelashes—jumped up from a chair behind a velvet-topped table.

"Hey, Maddy," Ethan said.

Maddy beamed. And then her eyes rested on me, and her face fell. "Who's this?" she asked, her voice tight.

Ethan touched my elbow. "This is Jesse."

"That's a boy's name," Maddy said.

I furrowed my brow. "Well, it *can* be . . ."

"Ethan," Maddy said sweetly. "You can sit across from me. And you." She glared at me. "Can sit there."

Ethan and I took our seats.

"So you're Ethan." A curly-haired girl dressed in fortune-teller garb that was less over-the-top than Maddy's stared across the table at him.

"Yes," Ethan said simply.

"I'm Brittany."

Ethan nodded. "Hey."

Brittany whispered something to Maddy, and Maddy giggled. Then she focused back at Ethan. "So. Do you want to go first, Ethan?"

Ethan glanced over at me.

"Go ahead," I said.

Ethan shrugged and rested his hand palm-up on the table.

"Okay." Maddy examined his palm closely, her cheeks turning pink. "I am going to look at three lines. Life, success, and love. Let's start with your life line . . . Wow, it's very strong."

"That's good, right?" Ethan said.

Maddy nodded. "Totes. It means you're going to live a long and productive life."

Ethan looked over at me and nodded satisfactorily.

"Now. Let's take a look at your success line." Maddy paused for a moment. "This line is perfect and unbroken. That means you're going to be very successful. I'm guessing you'll write a movie that's bigger than *Twilight* and buy a big house and a nice car, like a Jeep Grand Cherokee."

Ethan grinned. "Sounds good to me."

Maddy fluttered her long lashes. "I'm not surprised. You're very talented."

"Next, I'm going to look at your love line." Maddy's lips curled up in a smile. "I see here you're going to find the perfect girl."

Ethan glanced over at me for a tiny, electrically charged second.

"But not for a long time," Maddy said quickly. "It looks like she's going to be a few years younger than you. Which is good because then she won't get all old and wrinkly for a long time." She shot me a look.

Ethan stared at his hand. "Hmm."

"So. What do you think?" Maddy asked, eyes on Ethan.

"I think it sounds like I have a lot to look forward to."

"Yep." Maddy smiled. Then she turned to me. "I guess you're next," she grumbled.

"It's my turn to do it," Brittany said.

"Can you let me?" Maddy asked.

"No. We're supposed to take turns."

"I'll give you my Victoria's Secret lotion."

"Fine."

I rested my hand on the table, nerves building inside. In my mind I knew I was in a tent at a middle school carnival, waiting for a twelve-year-old to look at my life, success, and love lines, but my heart was still beating kind of fast.

Maddy stared down at my hand. "Oh," she said flatly.

"What?" I asked, leaning forward.

"I'm seeing something strange in your heart line."

"What?"

"See how it's all choppy?"

I looked down. "Not really."

"Well, it is. And that means you'll chase love, like, a ton of times, but it will never work out. Ever."

I narrowed my eyes, staring at the lines in my palm.

"But maybe your success line is better."

"Okay." Brow furrowed, I looked over at Ethan, who was smiling amusedly at how wrapped up I was getting in my reading.

"Uh-oh." Maddy bit her lip.

"It's not better?"

"Actually, it's worse." She sighed. "You're never really going to amount to anything."

"That is so sad," Brittany said without looking up from a text she was busy composing.

Maddy shot her friend a glare. "But don't worry. I've never seen anyone who has a bad love, success, and life line."

"Oh. Good."

Maddy shifted in her seat and looked down at my hand. And then she gasped dramatically.

"What?" Brittany asked, eyes wide.

"This life line is the shortest I've ever seen." Maddy frowned. "You're going to die young. And it's not going to be pretty. I'm seeing signs in your health line of a flesh-eating virus."

Brittany covered her mouth with her hand. "Gross."

"It will start out by making you hideous-looking. Then you'll start to smell. And then you'll die." Maddy shot Ethan a "think about it" look.

Wait a minute . . .

I stared across the table at Maddy, the dots beginning to connect in my mind. Of course! Maddy was Maggie—the girl Rosa overheard Ethan talking about!

"Well," I said with a sigh. "I can't believe all the bad news I've gotten today."

"Sorry." Maddy shrugged. "At least no man will have to look at your puss-encrusted scab body."

I stood up from my seat. "I guess you're right."

"Hey!" the girl at the entrance called into the tent. "Are you ready for two more?"

"Sure," Brittany called back. "Let me do it this time, Maddy."

Ethan got up and walked behind me to the tent door.

"Bye, Ethan," Maddy said. "Thanks for coming to my booth."

Ethan nodded. "Thanks for reading my palm."

Maddy and Brittany whispered and giggled some more as Ethan and I exited the booth and rejoined the noise and energy of the carnival.

"Wow," I said with a grin. "Looks like I have some competition."

Ethan shrugged. "I guess the ladies can't get enough."

I laughed as my lips curved up into a flirty smile. "I'd say that's a pretty accurate statement."

Ethan looked into my eyes for a moment, then reached out and laced his fingers through mine.

"Now where to?" I asked, enjoying the warmth of his hand, the way it seemed to run up my fingers and through my whole body.

"Wherever we want."

We spent the next couple hours exploring the carnival. We

stopped at a face-painting booth where I got a heart on one cheek and a peace sign on the other, and Ethan got half his face painted blue, *Braveheart*-style. We fished for "Say No to Drugs," "Math is Cool," and "Stop the Spitballs" stickers at a fishing booth. We rode on the most rickety Ferris wheel in the world. We bought a funnel cake that made me feel sick to my stomach.

It was fantastic.

We were weaving through the vendor booths—filled with jewelry, glassware, and other trinkets—when I spotted a T-shirt in the $5 T-shirt booth. It was bright yellow and featured a weird-looking potato chip man and the words "Happy National Potato Chip Day!"

I had to have it.

I pulled Ethan toward the booth, pointed out the shirt, and moved to hand the vendor my five dollars. But Ethan beat me to the punch. I thanked him with a hug and slipped the shirt on right over my clothes.

"So." Ethan shot me an intrigued look as we walked away. "National Potato Chip Day?"

I smoothed down my awesome new shirt. "Yeah. It's on Monday."

"How do you know that?"

I watched as two little girls ran past, balloons tied to their wrists. "Ever since I was little, I've had a really big thing for holidays. And I always hated waiting months in between the big ones to celebrate. Then after my dad died, I decided to celebrate as often as possible. So I keep a calendar with pretty much every holiday imaginable on it. If I see a day I'd like to celebrate, I do."

"Well." Ethan gently bumped the side of his body into mine. "I'll keep that in mind."

A soft, fizzy feeling moved up my limbs, and I reveled in it as we tried on trucker hats, looked for our names on keychains, and listened as a guy tried to convince us to buy jumbo belt buckles.

We were walking hand in hand toward the exit gates, when I spotted something that made me stop.

Goldfish.

About ten of them swimming in glass bowls inside a red, white, and blue booth. I'd seen the game at lots of carnivals before. And I'd always wondered something.

I pulled Ethan in the direction of the fish and asked the kid manning the booth: "What happens to the goldfish that nobody wins?"

The kid looked at me like I was dense. "They get flushed."

That was all I needed to hear. I reached into Ethan's hoodie pocket and grabbed out the few tickets we had left. I handed them to the kid in exchange for five ping-pong balls. I tossed the balls, aiming for the little bowls.

But when I was done, I hadn't won a single goldfish.

I quickly ran to a nearby ticket booth and bought a bunch more tickets. I tossed. Ethan tossed. And twelve bucks later, we'd won two of the goldfish. I was seriously starting to worry that we wouldn't be able to save all the fish.

"What are we going to do?" I asked Ethan.

"Can we buy the fish?" Ethan asked the kid.

"Nope."

"Come on." I stared at the kid and remembered Maddy. Maybe a little reminder that I was a hot older woman would help. "Are you sure you don't want to help us out?" I asked in a husky voice.

"Listen, lady. I have a girlfriend. A hot one. And I couldn't help you if I wanted to. Something about taxes."

I looked at Ethan, panic in my face.

He glanced around, as if searching for a solution. And then he took off running.

I watched his back, wondering if he'd decided I was too crazy for him.

But thankfully, he returned a moment later with a group of kids.

"This is Robbie," he said, pointing to the tallest boy in the group. "He's the pitcher for the Trinity Prep baseball team."

Robbie nodded at me.

"I'm going to pay him two bucks for every fish he wins," Ethan said.

My mouth turned into a huge smile as Robbie turned his hat backwards, and started tossing ping-pong balls like it was nothing. I watched in complete glee as he won one fish. Then two. Then three.

Before I knew it, the kid running the booth was handing me all nine goldfish, swimming happily in plastic bags; Ethan was handing Robbie twenty bucks; and the girls Robbie was with were looking at him like he was a hero.

I was positively giddy, holding my cute little friends on my lap as Ethan drove me home.

"How did you think of asking that kid to play the game for us?" I asked Ethan.

"I can get pretty creative when I want something." He looked over at me intently.

"I see," I said in reply.

And suddenly, an idea came to my mind.

nine

"Hey, Magda?"

My boss looked up from the register, where she was refilling the dimes. "Yeah?"

"Mind if I hang this flyer for my art class on the bulletin board out front?" I held up the light blue flyer I'd worked on over the weekend. "I'm adding something new, something I really hope will save the class, and I just want to get the word out."

Magda slammed the register shut. "Sure. Let me just . . . go clear a space on the board."

"It's okay," I said, grabbing the stapler from beneath the counter. "I can do it."

Magda pushed past me and practically ran outside.

What in the world?

I quickened my pace to keep up with her, and when I got to the bulletin board, I saw her covering up a poster with one hand while simultaneously trying to remove it with the other.

"What is that?" I asked, reaching for it.

Magda fought me off, crumpling the sheet up, which made me want to see it even more. So I grabbed it out of her hand and turned my back on her, quickly un-crumpling it.

When I saw what it was, my mouth fell open.

There, on the poster, was a photo of me in my waitress apron, standing behind the counter. Below the photo were these words:

Sugar House Coffee Employee of the Month
Name: Jesse
Age: 31
Favorite Movies: Yellow Submarine, White Christmas
Favorite Bands: Sufjan Stevens, Death Cab for Cutie
Favorite Foods: Creamsicles, Gardenburgers
Sign: Libra
Status: Single

"What?" I reread the last line, hoping I'd read it wrong. But I hadn't.

"Surprise!" Magda said. "You're the new Employee of the Month!"

I narrowed my eyes. "You don't even have an Employee of the Month."

"Now I do!" Magda held her arms out in the air like she was presenting me a gift.

"So that's why everyone's been congratulating me," I said to myself. Then I looked at Magda. "I can't belief you put all this stuff on here. Are you crazy?"

"I just thought the customers would like some facts about our Employee of the Month," Magda said innocently.

"Stop saying that," I said. "You know I'm not Employee of the Month."

"Yes, you are."

"Okay, then. What do I get? A day off? Free muffins? A bonus check?"

Magda waved a hand in the air. "Fine. You're not."

I stared down at the poster in my hand, brow furrowed. "This thing is professionally made."

"Kinkos," Magda said.

Oh, brother.

"I just thought after last week when you gave your number . . ." Magda softened her voice. I could tell she was going to use her trump card. "I just want you to be happy, sweetie."

Yep. There it was.

"Well . . ." I said with a sigh, "now that you bring it up, I actually started seeing . . . someone."

"Really?" Magda asked, eyes wide with intrigue.

I smiled as I put the crumpled poster in a nearby trashcan and stapled my flyer to the board. Then without another word, I moved back into the café. "See you later, Magda. I'm off to class."

"Wait!" she called after me. "That's all you're going to give me? Come on, Jesse!"

---> ◆ <---

"Hi, everyone! Welcome to Yogainting!"

The members of my class stared at me, standing in front of the room in my ripped Shins T-shirt, leggings, and '80s sweatband.

"What?" they asked practically in unison.

"Yogainting!" I repeated. "Yoga plus Painting."

The idea started after the carnival, when Ethan mentioned being creative to get what you want. I got home that night and looked up the classes Darla said were successful at the center.

All of them had one thing in common: They combined more than one activity.

Pilates + Boxing = Piloxing.

Kranking + Spinning = Krankinning.

Scrapbooking + Blogging = Scrogging.

So I came up with the idea to combine my class with something else.

Yoga + Painting = Yogainting.

"What in the world are you talking about," Eldon's voice

came into my ears. "You are at your painting class. I'm Eldon. Do you know what date it is?"

"I'm fine, Eldon," I said.

"Didn't you get the email she sent?" Gladys asked him.

Eldon grumbled. "Email? I don't have email. I have a CB radio."

"The email said to wear workout clothes," Jana explained.

"And you sure look pretty in yours," Jerome said.

Jana gritted her teeth.

"If you're in regular clothes, you'll be fine," I said to Eldon.

"But I thought we were painting using our photos as inspiration?" Eldon asked.

"We still are. But we're adding a little twist. Something to help us get even deeper." I narrowed my eyes for effect. "Okay. Let's begin. Please stand."

"Do you think you can get up?" Terry asked Bill angrily. "Or does that require actual initiative?"

Bill sighed and stood up.

I turned on the Yogainting mix CD I'd spent a few hours making last night. Some Kings of Convenience, a little Red House Painters.

Jana hopped out of her seat. "This is cool!"

"You're cool," Jerome said.

"I don't know if I should do this." Gladys grimaced as she stood. "My pinky toe has really been hurting."

"Just do what you can." I took a deep breath. Here we go. "Let's begin in Mountain Pose. And as we do, we'll think of our inspiration."

I demonstrated the pose and the class mimicked me.

"Okay. Now we're going to add painting." My voice was soft and low. "Pick up a paintbrush."

The class picked up their brushes.

"We're going to stand in Tree Pose for four counts while we paint. Then we're going to switch legs." I showed the class what to do. "Okay. Select a color from your palette. And Tree Pose.

And paint, two, three, four. And switch legs. And paint, two, three, four."

Jana smiled broadly as she held a perfect Tree Pose. "This is kind of fun!"

"You're kind of fun," Jerome said.

Jana rolled her eyes. "Ugh."

"It's not fun, it's crazy," Eldon said as he fumbled with his paintbrush while trying to stay balanced.

"It's not crazy!" I said a little too loudly. Then I lowered my voice again. "It's the future."

"Does this have something to do with that blonde who was here last time?" Eldon asked.

I looked out at the class. "Well . . . maybe a little . . ."

Eldon shook his head. "I knew I didn't trust her. She was definitely up to something. I'm pretty sure she had a camera in her left earring."

"If she did, she caught Jana looking gorgeous that day," Jerome said.

"Jerome!" Jana begged.

"How could there have been a camera in her earring?" Bill asked. "They were tiny diamond studs."

"Are you kidding me?" Terry snapped her head toward her husband.

"What?" Bill asked.

Terry pointed her paintbrush at her husband. "What did I wear yesterday?"

Bill frowned, deep lines forming in his forehead. "Something . . . blue? Oh, I know. That sweater with the frogs on it."

"They're turtles!" Terry snapped. "See this is your problem, Bill. You don't—"

"Is this Yogainting?" Two super-fit girls came into the room, gym bags over their shoulders.

They must've seen one of the flyers I put up around the neighborhood! My plan was working! I just might be able to save the class after all!

"Yes, it is," I said cheerily. And then I bowed and whispered, "Namaste."

I basked in my success as I led the class through more poses and painting. Soon the class was gone, and I was cleaning up a few stray palettes and brushes.

I was rinsing out some brushes when I heard the sound of the door latch. I looked over, expecting to see a class member who forgot something. But instead I saw a handsome, solid figure I immediately recognized.

Troy.

My heart beat a little faster at the sight of him.

"Hey, teach," he said, approaching me.

I turned off the water. "You came."

"I said I would, didn't I?"

I wiped my hands on a towel and noticed I could feel my heavy pulse. "I suppose you did."

"What are you doing right now?" Troy asked, a bold glint in his eye.

I blinked, meeting his gaze. "I don't really have any plans."

"Well," Troy took hold of my hand, "you do now."

ten

"When was the last time you went golfing?" Troy asked as he maneuvered our golf cart toward Hole 1.

"Does miniature golfing count?" I asked.

Troy laughed like it was a cute little joke.

And that, my friend, should have been my first clue.

"I love it out here." Troy parked the cart and slid off the seat, all smooth and athletic. "I try to come as much as I can."

I adjusted my cropped khakis and the polo shirt I borrowed from David and kept in step with Troy like I was a regular golf expert, and not the girl who'd never been on a real golf course before.

The caddies—two teenage boys, Carter and Ryan—followed behind us.

"Ladies first," Troy said.

I bit my lip nervously. "Oh, really? Okay."

I moved toward Ryan, who was holding the bag of clubs Troy had rented for me in the Pro Shop, and searched for the correct club to use.

I'm not going to lie, I thought they'd have helpful markings on them. Like: "Tee Off" or "Use me for Putting" or something like that.

But all I could see were numbers.

And weird ones. Like 3 and 5 and 9.

I kept my eye on Ryan, and grabbed a slim club out of the bag. He frowned. So I slowly lowered it. Then I raised another one and watched. He frowned again. I did this two more times, and when Ryan nodded in approval, I smiled like I'd finally found what I was looking for.

Ryan handed me a pink golf ball and tee, and with a deep breath, I moved toward the tee zone or whatever it's called. I put the tee in the ground and set the ball atop it. Then I got in position, closed my eyes, and swung.

The club made a whooshing sound in the air as it missed the ball completely.

But that's not all.

Due to the momentum, I spun around, doing a full-on 180-degree turn.

I took a quick glance over my shoulder to see that both caddies were forcing back smiles, and Troy was grinning like he found it adorable.

"Okay!" I said as I got back into position. "Now that I did my lucky move, time to golf it up!"

I smiled at Troy before trying again.

It was the last smile to appear on my face for the next hour and a half.

Why?

Because I freaking hate golf!

I'm sorry if golf is your one true love, or if you went to college on a golf scholarship, or if the only time your grandfather ever told you he loved you was when you were playing golf, but it's a horrible, horrible game!

Here are just a few things I don't get about it:

- The tees: If everyone—your caddy, other golfers, the groundskeeper—is going to give you a hard time when you take a few chunks out of the grass, then why are the tees so tiny? If you don't want people to dig up the grass with their clubs—then how about a tee that sits higher off the ground? Eight inches, maybe? It's basic math, people!

- The clubs: Nine iron. Three wood. Putter. Pitching wedge. Lob Wedge. Ultra Lob Wedge. It's too much, I tell you! Too much!
- The scoring: I don't know why Ryan made such a big deal when I celebrated after he told me I had the highest score after three holes. Last I heard high scores were good, Ryan.
- Those blasted sand traps: They're just mean.
- Which brings me to: The rule against throwing the ball out of the sand traps.

I wiped some sweat from my brow with my sleeve and hit the ball again. Sand went everywhere. In my eyes. In my ears. In my mouth.

All I wanted to do was pick up that ball up and throw it.

But I didn't.

Finally, by some miracle, I hit the thing out of the trap and then onto the green. Five shots later, it went into the little tin cup and made that glorious sound I can still sometimes hear when I'm falling asleep at night.

"Par plus twelve," Ryan said.

Troy put an arm around me. "Nice putt."

I couldn't help but laugh. "I am pretty amazing."

I enjoyed the feeling of Troy's arm around me as we made our way back to the cart and sped off to Hole 9.

When we reached it, I took a little breather and just watched Troy golf. His arm muscles flexing as he swung. His tan neck accentuated by the collar of his shirt. His long legs bending in amazing ways.

Carter and Ryan talked and joked with Troy as he made perfect shot after perfect shot. I'd started to notice that Troy had that effect on people—they liked him immediately.

Soon Troy's ball was a few feet away from the green.

"Dude," Carter said. "I think you have a shot at the birdie."

The birdie?

Frowning, I looked out at the grass in front of us, and suddenly my stomach dropped. On the opposite side of the green, was a pretty little bird, hopping around, minding its own business.

"I think you're right," I heard Troy say.

What?

I stared at him, brow furrowed in worry. No way was he going to hit a living creature with a golf ball.

"Ten bucks if you hit it," Carter said.

"You're on!"

Disbelief and panic rose up in my chest as Troy got into his stance. I looked at him. I looked at the bird. And then he swung his club back.

"No!!!" I flung myself at him, grabbing the club with all my might. And then I called out to the bird. "Fly away, little birdie. Find a safe zone!"

Heart racing, I watched as the bird hopped around for a moment and then flew away.

It was as my breath returned to normal, and everyone stared at me like I was crazy, that I remembered something.

Playing Wii Golf with Uncle Logan.

And hearing the electronic voice on the game say . . . "Nice birdie!"

Oh no.

"Um . . ." I stammered, staring at the ground. "I just . . . I thought . . ."

Troy put a white-gloved hand on my shoulder. "What do you say we skip the back nine and head in for some dinner?"

I hid my face in my hands as we made our way to the golf cart. "Promise me you're not going to tell anyone about that."

"I try not to make promises I have absolutely no intention of keeping. I'm old-fashioned that way."

···→ ◆ ←···

Now this . . . is more like it.

Dipping a perfect grilled cheese into a delicious tomato bisque, enjoying the distant tinkling of a piano, and staring at the hottest guy in the room—way better than golf.

"You were a real sport out there," Troy said as he cut into his salmon.

I took a sip of my water. "Golf is hard! How come no one ever tells you how hard it is?"

"Because then we wouldn't be able to convince you to play with us."

I felt the corners of my mouth move up.

"Thanks for coming, Jesse. I tried to play it cool and make it to the weekend. But I really wanted to see you."

"Thanks for bringing me." I held up my sandwich. "This is the best grilled cheese I've ever had."

Troy nodded. "It's the sourdough. They fly it in from San Francisco."

"San Francisco." I sighed. "I love it there. It's on my list of top four places I'd like to live. Along with Portland, Seattle, and Denver."

"That list is a lot different than your top-four-places-to-visit list."

"Oh, yeah," I said. "I look for totally different things in a place I'd visit versus a place I'd live."

Troy leaned toward me. "Tell me more."

I flashed him a coy grin. "Well, in a place to live I want: bike paths, good farmers markets, art, music, theater, some kind of water nearby. In a place to visit: snow."

Troy nodded and picked up his glass.

"But there is one exception to the snow rule," I continued.

"And what is that?"

"Australia."

"Good exception," Troy said. "Australia is amazing."

"You've been there?"

"Two summers ago. For a scuba diving trip."

"Well, I'm going to go someday." I tucked one of my legs under me. "On January 26."

Troy furrowed his brow, his eyes sparkling. "Someday? Or January 26?"

"January 26 is Australia Day. So, sometime, in the future, I will go to Australia, as long as it's on January 26."

Troy looked intrigued. "Australia Day, huh?"

I leaned back in my seat. "Yeah. I'm kind of obsessed with obscure holidays."

"Which ones have you celebrated lately?" Troy asked.

"Well, March 2 was Old Things Day, so I wore my favorite vintage Beatles T-shirt to work and visited the Natural History Museum and looked at dinosaur bones. And March 12 was Alfred Hitchcock day, so Laurel and I watched *Rear Window*, *Vertigo*, and *Psycho*, and then she stayed the night because she was too scared to drive home."

Troy tilted his glass, the ice cubes clinking together. "What's today?"

"National Quilting Day and National Poultry Day," I said. "But I don't eat meat, and I can barely sew on a button so—"

"Troy?"

I looked up and saw none other than the woman from the photo in Troy's office standing beside our table, looking like Golfing Barbie in her perfectly fitting khakis and white polo shirt.

"Vivian?" Troy said. "What are you doing here?"

"I thought a round might help me relax. I've been stressing about our meeting with the FCC guy tomorrow."

Our meeting?

"Vivian, this is Jesse." Troy brushed his hand against my shoulder. My skin instantly got all tingly. "Jesse, this is my business partner, Vivian."

Suddenly it all clicked into place. Vivian Kline. Of Parker/Kline Creative. Troy's business partner of four years.

"Hi," I said with a wave.

"Hello, Jesse." Vivian's words were perfectly polished. Like she'd gone to the best schools and taken all the right classes. "I don't mean to interrupt, but would it be okay if I sat with you until my driver gets here?"

"Um . . ." Troy looked over at me.

"Of course," I said quickly.

"*Merci beaucoup.*" Vivian sat down, her back straight like a ballet dancer, and brushed a strand of her cascading, Isla Fisher–red hair out of her face with nails painted in a pale pink.

I was instantly aware of my slouchy posture, messy braided buns, and beat up nails covered in traces of the blue, black, and purple paint I was using in a current art project.

"So did you have a good day on the course?" Vivian asked after beckoning the waiter for "Vichy water, *s'il vous plait.*"

"Golf is not my game," I said with a laugh. "But Troy was amazing."

Vivian smiled at Troy as if agreeing with me. "Oh, well. Some people just aren't made for golf. It's a very specialized sport."

"Yeah." I frowned. "I guess so."

"I think you did great." Troy reached out and gently touched my fingertips.

Vivian sat up straighter and smiled a sorority-girl smile. "I like your braids, Jesse. Very . . . bohemian."

Is it just me, or can you hear another translation behind her words?

Like this: I'm disgusted by your braids, Jesse. Very . . . bum off the street.

I played with the spoon in my soup. "I like bohemian."

"I'm surprised Troy couldn't talk you into the salmon," Vivian said, eyeing my food. "It's *magnifique.*"

"Oh," I let go of the spoon, "I don't eat meat."

Vivian looked me over. "Well, good for you. It's carbs I try to stay away from."

Did you hear it that time?

Translation: Well, that's dumb. If you laid off the bread, you could be glorious like me.

"I like a girl who cares about animals." Troy touched my knee under the table.

"Oh, yeah. Animal lovers are great." Vivian cleared her throat. "So what do you do, Jesse?"

I took a sip of water. "I'm a waitress at a coffee shop."

"How exciting!" Vivian plastered on a smile. "I've always thought that looked like such . . . fun!"

I know you heard that one.

Translation: How lame! I've always thought that looked like . . . something a monkey could do!

"I really like it," I said with a nod.

"She also teaches art at the city center," Troy said, looking at me like I was the only girl at the table.

"The city center?" Vivian said. "Didn't they just bust up a meth lab in that building?"

"That was in the basement!" I said quickly.

Vivian raised her eyebrows. "I see."

The waiter returned with Vivian's water, and she sipped it through a long straw.

I did not wish he'd accidentally spilled it all over her.

"So, Troy, how did you and Vivian get into business together?" I asked.

"We met at Penn," Vivian answered for him. "Freshman year."

"Oh. So you guys go way back."

"We sure do." Vivian reached out and touched Troy's arm. "We dated all through school. But we realized we're much better as friends. We were both working at different ad agencies when we ran into each other at an event and hatched the idea of our own agency. For some reason, life just keeps bringing us together."

And with that, Vivian gave Troy a look that was a whole lot like the one I saw in the picture hanging on his office wall.

eleven

Thursday night. Family dinner.

"Your aunt kicked me out of the living room," Logan said as he came into the kitchen. "She said I should be helping you."

I set an orange pepper on the counter in front of him—because, as always, I was in charge of salad, the only thing I can really make. "Excellent. Grab a knife."

"She told me she wants you to help!" Logan yelled out to Linda, who was in the dining room setting the table.

"Don't believe his lies!" I called out even louder.

"I never do!" Linda hollered back.

"So how was your art class tonight?" Logan asked me.

"Actually, pretty good," I said as I chopped a cucumber. "We had two more people join."

Laurel came into the room and plopped down on a barstool on the other side of the counter. "Are you whining about your class again?"

"No."

She grabbed a grape tomato, the stack of bangles on her wrist jangling together. "I think I might have a solution for you."

I narrowed my eyes, wary of Laurel's "solution."

"I'm serious." Laurel popped the tomato in her mouth. "This lady came into the store today and told the personal shoppers she's on the board of a chain of fancy fine arts schools, and they're looking for music, dance, and art teachers."

I set down the Cutco knife I was using. "That actually sounds interesting."

Laurel shook her head. "Why does no one trust me?"

I wiped my hands on a towel, and Laurel handed me her phone, which was open to a Craigslist ad.

Exciting job opportunity for art teachers! Alive Academy of the Arts is seeking teachers in the following subjects: Music, dance, art
Hours: Monday-Friday 8:00 a.m. to 5:00 p.m.
Locations: Hill Pointe, PA; Brooklyn, NY; Chicago, IL; Austin, TX; Portland, OR
Applicants must be: creative, energetic, nurturing, and detail-oriented. Must have a Bachelor's degree in the subject to be taught or a Bachelor's degree in any subject plus 1 year of teaching experience
Interested parties should email resumes to Claire Overton: coverton@aliveacadamy.web

"This is full time," I said, looking up at Laurel. "What about Sugar House?"

Laurel's face didn't move. "I hate to tell you, but I'm sure Magda would be delighted if you got something else. You're a creative type. Waitressing . . . well, you're terrible at it."

"Hey. I happen to be Employee of the Month!"

Laurel rolled her eyes. "Please."

I sighed. "Fine."

"Anyway," Laurel continued, "the lady said something about there only being one opening here in Hill Pointe for an art teacher. So if I were you, I'd send your resume over tonight."

"I will." I kissed Laurel on the cheek and handed back the phone. "Thanks."

"So," Logan said, "now that we've talked about work . . ."

I shot him a tread-lightly look.

"David tells me your love life has taken a recent leap in activity."

I got back to chopping my cucumber. "You could say that."

Logan's brow furrowed. "You sound like you think it's a bad thing."

"You know I've never been Dating Girl. This is all so . . . foreign to me. And so much has changed. I don't know what I'm supposed to do. How much I'm supposed to tell . . ."

Logan looked at me intently. "No one ever said you have to reveal everything to every guy you date."

I frowned. "I know. But . . ."

Laurel grabbed another tomato. "But you want to, because you're a chronic over-sharer."

"I am not."

"Fourth grade." Laurel chewed the tomato. "You went to the nurse's office with a sore throat, and when she asked you how you thought you got it, you burst into tears and told her you put your Flintstones vitamin under your tongue in the morning so your mom would think you took it, and then spit it down the drain."

I lifted my chin in the air. "I don't know what you're talking about."

"Listen," Laurel said, "you're not doing anything wrong. You got burned by Jerk Nicholson, and of course you're going to do things differently than if you hadn't."

I chopped the same piece of cucumber over and over.

Was I always going to be this way? Confused? Scared?

"I think Laurel's right," Logan said.

"Thank you." Laurel got up from the stool and disappeared into the dining room.

"Just give yourself some time," Logan said kindly. "There's nothing wrong with taking it slow."

I placed the veggies in the glass bowl on the counter. "Yeah. This coming from a guy who told me he fell in love with Aunt Linda the first time he laid eyes on her."

"That's different. For me, one girl was all it took. I hit the jackpot the first time I took the gamble." Logan stared into the distance for a moment, as if remembering something.

I tossed the salad lightly. "So how did you know she was it . . . you know, The One?"

Logan met my eyes. "She inspired me."

I smiled a small smile and carried the salad bowl into the dining room, where Laurel was sitting at the table, texting away on her phone.

"Hey, guys!" David walked in, carrying a box of Spry gum for Linda and Logan, per usual.

"Oh, look," Laurel said, "it's one of the extras from *Lord of the Rings*."

"Oh, look," David said back, "it's one of the cast members of *Desperate Spinsters of Pennsylvania*."

We all took a seat around the table and poured our drinks. We were about to start serving up the food when Laurel cleared her throat. "Okay, guys. I have to tell you something. I invited someone over for dinner."

"Really?" Linda asked excitedly.

"His name is Clint. We've been . . . seeing each other for a few weeks now. And he wanted to meet you." She paused to look at David. "Well, not you, but whatever. Anyway, I was talking to my self-actualization guy, and he said that if I wanted tonight to go well, I needed to put into the universe exactly how I want it to go."

David coughed.

"So . . . I made these lists for you guys. Things I want you to talk about."

Everyone was silent as Laurel handed each of us a 3x5 card.

Things to Mention to Clint:
- My love of children and animals
- My concern for the environment
- My five-days-a-week workout regimen
- My volunteer work
- My lack of materialism

Logan and Linda exchanged glances.

I kept my head down, staring at the card, waiting.

"You've got to be kidding me."

And there it was.

"What, David?" Laurel asked, fixing him with a glare.

"Your love of children and animals? What do you want me to tell him about first? The time you vacuumed up Snowball the gerbil—"

"Hey!" Laurel protested. "I thought he was a pile of cotton balls. I told you that!"

David continued, unfazed, "—or the time you told the Girl Scouts selling cookies to get lost because if you wanted to buy overpriced cookies you'd go to Dean and Deluca."

Laurel looked to her parents for backup.

Linda cleared her throat. "Could you maybe . . . tell us what you were meaning by these? For example, your concern for the environment, that would be referring to . . . ?" Linda tried to come up with something, but couldn't.

Laurel folded her arms across her chest. "It could refer to any number of things. Like the time I . . . tossed my Sprite can into the recycling bin when we were camping in the Poconos last summer."

"Because it was closer," I said before I could stop myself.

Laurel shot me a death look.

"Sorry." I clamped my lips shut.

"How about the workout regimen?" Linda asked. "I thought you said sweating is for farmers."

"I walk!" Laurel said. "My office is on the second floor and sometimes the escalator and the elevator are broken."

Linda nodded. "Oh. Okay."

Ding. Dong.

"That's him," Laurel said, standing up. "Could you just . . . try? And hide your cards."

We all moved our cards out of view.

David shook his head in disbelief.

We listened as Laurel greeted a man with a nice, deep voice and then brought him into the dining room.

"Everyone," she said, resting on the arm of a tall, muscular guy, "this is Clint."

"It's nice to meet you, Clint." Logan stood up from his seat and shook Clint's hand.

Clint handed a bouquet of flowers to Linda, who cooed over how lovely they were and then told him to sit and please help himself to something to drink, some salad, and some lasagna.

Clint obliged.

"So, Clint," I said, the first to try to help Laurel reach self-actualization, or whatever. "I'm surprised Laurel could fit you in during the week, what with her intense training schedule."

Clint looked over at Laurel, eyebrows raised. "Training?"

"Oh, yes," I said, sounding a bit like a car saleswoman. "We barely see her. She's going to be in the . . . marathon."

Clint looked almost hurt. "I asked you if you wanted to train with me and you said you would, but you were busy with yoga."

"That's what I mean," I said quickly. "The yoga marathon."

Clint cocked his head to one side.

I nodded. "Oh, yeah. The last one to fall asleep wins."

David let out a grunt slash snort.

"I just thought of something!" Aunt Linda said suddenly.

All eyes went to her.

"One time when we went shopping, Laurel convinced me to get a jumbo bottle of Head and Shoulders. I haven't had to buy any for almost a year now."

"I think what she's saying," I said as if to the whole table, though we all knew it was for Clint, "is that Laurel is a real environmentalist."

"Thank goodness." Clint looked at Laurel the way all the guys she dates do, like she had him under a spell. "I'm an environmental lawyer, and being with someone like-minded is very important to me."

"So I guess you like animals then too, huh?" I asked.

Clint nodded. "I volunteer at a shelter every weekend that I don't have to work."

"Well, Laurel . . ." I paused, searching my brain for a good Laurel + animal story. But all I could think of was poor little Snowball. "Laurel . . . has a dog."

Laurel's mouth dropped open.

"Sorry," I mouthed.

"Really?" Clint said. "How come I've never seen your dog?"

Laurel shot me a Fix-it look.

"Did I say dog?" I said, laughing. "I meant frog. She had a frog. But then I took this Creole cooking class. And I was supposed to make something authentic for the class. But I forgot to go to the store. So . . ."

Clint looked at me with complete disgust.

Ah, well. I wasn't trying to date him.

I glanced across the table and saw Linda looking down at her index card. After a second she looked up. "So, Clint? Do you volunteer anywhere other than the animal shelter?"

"The soup kitchen," he said as he speared a tomato with his fork. "And the Boys & Girls Club."

"Laurel likes to volunteer too," Linda said. But, notice, she didn't elaborate.

"Oh, yeah," David deadpanned. "We call her Laurel Teresa."

"She really is a gem," Linda said. "But she doesn't have any gems. Or anything materialistic, really. One time I left a hundred-dollar bill on the table, and she just walked right by it."

"She is something special," Clint said.

Laurel beamed.

And as I looked at the two of them, I totally understood.

Understood the desire to put your best foot forward, even if it meant holding some things back.

I stared down at the index card in my lap. If only I had a list like that for my situation. Something simple and straightforward to tell me exactly what to reveal.

But I didn't.

And I had absolutely no clue.

twelve

"Happy Waffle Day!"

I looked onto my doorstep where Ethan stood—dressed in jeans, a tee and hoodie, and black Converse—holding a bottle of maple syrup with a big yellow bow tied to it.

"Oh, my goodness." A warm, happy feeling bubbled up inside of me. "You looked up what day it is."

When Ethan called last night to ask me out, he was being cryptic about what he had planned, and I could tell he really wanted to tell me. This, I never would have guessed.

"Yes, I did. Now. Put that away." Ethan handed me the syrup. "And then grab a jacket. I'm taking you downtown."

"For what?" I asked as I set the syrup on the kitchen counter.

"You'll see." Ethan shoved his hands in his pockets and looked over at David, who was on the couch playing a video game.

"Hey," Ethan said to David.

"Hey," David said back.

I grabbed my jacket and bag and said good-bye to my brother.

Ethan asked how my day was as we walked to the corner

where his car was parked at a meter. He opened my door for me and waited until I was situated before slamming it shut. When he got into the driver's seat and started up the car, I instantly tuned the radio to my favorite station.

I liked that he let me.

That was the thing about Ethan. He made me feel like I could just . . . be. Like he wouldn't mind if I changed his radio station. Like he would be cool if I said I liked the Yankees better than the Phillies. Like he'd bring me soup when I was sick and in my pajamas and still tell me I looked pretty.

I seat-danced to one of my favorite Iron & Wine songs as we drove and talked about my adventures at Sugar House and the city center and his adventures in trying to get the pool ready for the summer.

"So did you send your resume to that art academy you told me about last night?" he asked, looking over at me as he drove, one hand on the wheel, one hand holding mine.

"I sure did."

"Do you want the job?"

I pulled my right knee up to my chest. "Well. I researched the academy online. It looks pretty cool."

"Then I hope you get it."

Ethan turned on his blinker and pulled into a parking garage.

I tried to figure out where we were but had no idea. All I saw was a bank, a dry cleaner, and a vitamin store.

After parking in the garage, we walked into a building with shiny tile floors and generic white walls. Ethan looked more and more excited the longer we walked. I found his enthusiasm, and the fact that he'd gone to this trouble for me, so endearing.

Finally, we reached the end of a long hallway. A few people were congregated outside a room, and I spotted a sign beside the door:

Breakfast for Beginners

"A cooking class!" I beamed at Ethan.

It was such a unique idea. So creative. So off the beaten path. So Ethan.

Ethan took hold of my hand, and we walked into the room, which consisted of about twenty cooking stations, and found a spot in the back.

I looked at the utensils, pots and pans, and burners in front of me and decided this was the day I would finally learn to cook. This was the day . . .

Oh no.

I froze when I spotted the teacher entering the room.

I immediately recognized her as Mrs. Frye, the woman who taught my cooking class back in high school.

The class I told Ethan about.

The class that ruined cooking for me.

The class I may have had a teeny part in getting taken off the schedule.

And she was pretty mad about it, judging by the note I found in my locker.

What goes around comes around, Jesse Young.
Someday you will pay for the mess you've made.

I mean, I couldn't prove Mrs. Frye had written the note, but it was on stationery with "Parsley, Sage, Rosemary, and Thyme to Cook!" on the top, and "From the desk of C. Frye" on the bottom.

Suddenly I had a flashback to that day.

We were making pasta. I was trying to get my water to boil, and it just wasn't working. Everyone else's water was all bubbly, but mine was just . . . water. So, even though Mrs. Frye said to use medium heat, I turned my burner all the way up. And everything would have been fine if Suzy Martinez wasn't in front of me, flipping her hair around in an attempt to get Craig Winthrop's attention.

"Jesse?" Ethan's voice came into my ears. "You okay?"

"Yes." I shook my head as if to get the high-school thoughts out of there. "I'm great."

Mrs. Frye wouldn't recognize me. I was a grown woman now. Not the Radiohead T-shirt wearing kid with the blonde streak in her hair.

"Welcome!" Mrs. Frye said in her I'm-trying-to-sound-like-Julia-Child voice. "My name is Carol Frye, and I am your instructor."

Carol, huh? I would've pegged her as a Marge. Maybe a Norma.

"How many of you have ever watched someone cook something fabulous and thought to yourself, I could do that?"

A few people raised their hands.

Carol nodded. "How many of you have ever watched someone cook something fabulous and thought to yourself, I could never do that?"

A bunch of hands went into the air, including mine.

Ethan reached over and patted my shoulder.

"No matter what group you're in, you CAN learn to cook. Tonight we are going to make pancakes and waffles. We will start by making a multi-purpose batter. What's a batter?" Carol looked out at the class.

A few hands shot up.

But Carol ignored them. "I don't know," she said with a wide grin. "What's a batter with you?" She put her hand on her stomach and laughed hard.

Oh, man. More high school flashbacks.

"Let's begin by mixing our dry ingredients."

The classroom filled with the sound of chatter combined with that of pouring and stirring. I measured and mixed away, enjoying being near Ethan as I worked.

"The glass measuring cup is for the liquid ingredients."

I jumped when I heard Carol's voice.

I picked up a plastic cup and kept my head down. "Thank you, person I've never seen before in my life."

Carol frowned and made her way around the rest of the room.

When we finished mixing the dry ingredients, it was time to add the eggs, milk, and oil. It went without a hitch.

"I'm having a lot of fun," I said, poking Ethan with a flour-covered whisk.

He looked at me like there was nowhere else he'd rather be than here, cooking with me. "Me too."

"Okay, class," Carol said from the front of the room. "It's time to heat up our pans and get ready to pour our pancakes."

I'm not going to lie, I could feel my hands start to get clammy. I'm fine with food prep, but when it's time to actually cook—I tend to freak out.

"We will start by putting the stove to the pancake setting," Carol explained. "When your pan is hot, add a pat of butter to prevent the cakes from sticking."

I held my breath as Ethan turned the dial on his burner, dropped some butter into his pan, and stirred it around with a spatula.

I copied him exactly.

But while Ethan's butter started to melt, mine sat there in the pan, not changing at all.

I'm telling you, there's something wrong with me.

Determined to get that butter to melt, I decided to turn the heat up just a smidge.

A few seconds later, I noticed the butter started to melt. I smiled happily. Until . . .

It started to get brown.

I frowned and moved it around the pan with my spatula.

But it was getting darker brown.

And then almost black.

And then it started to smell. Bad.

Ethan looked over at me, brow furrowed, as did a few other people at nearby stations.

Carol, with her bloodhound-like cooking nose, immediately

rushed over to my station. "Oh, dear," she said, reaching across me. "Let's lower your temperature."

I looked up at her, a panicked expression on my face.

"And then we'll . . ." Carol narrowed her eyes suddenly. "Jesse Young?"

I shook my head. "Nope. Never heard of her."

Ethan frowned. "Wait. What—?"

I shook my head at him.

"You're not Jesse Young?" Carol asked.

"No. My name's . . . Elizabeth Hasselbeck."

I don't know. It was the only name that came to my mind.

Ethan looked completely confused as Carol reached into her pocket and retrieved a sheet of paper. "Well, that's strange. Because I don't have an Elizabeth Hasselbeck on my registration. I do, however, have a Jesse Young."

I opened my mouth to respond, but nothing came out.

Carol crossed her arms and fixed me with a hateful stare. "So we meet again."

I gulped.

"I've thought of this moment many times," she continued. "Thought of what I'd say to you. What I'd do."

My eyes got wide. Logically, I knew she wasn't going to do anything to me. But suddenly I was fifteen years old, watching the fire trucks rush into the school parking lot.

"Ethan," I whispered.

"Yeah?" he moved his ear toward my mouth.

"I'm going to say something, and I need you to just do it. Okay?"

"Okay . . ."

I quickly turned off our burners to make sure no fires would be started. "Run!"

---→ ◆ ←---

"So when you say you had a bad experience in a cooking class in high school you really mean it?"

I laughed and let the cool air wash over my face. We were out on the sidewalk, a block away from the cooking class, and I'd just finished telling Ethan why I made him run away from Breakfast for Beginners.

"Of course I did," I said. "You thought I was exaggerating?"

Ethan shrugged adorably. "Well . . ."

I playfully nudged him.

"Actually, now that I heard that whole story," he said. "I'm feeling kind of bad for subjecting you to that."

"Don't. It was fun." I put my arm through his and rested my head on his shoulder. All I wanted was to be near him. "So how is the writing coming?"

"You know," Ethan looked down at me, our eyes meeting, "pretty good. Better than it has in a long time, I think. I've started something new."

"Can I read it?"

"That depends. Are you going to tell me what you really think? Or are you one of those people who'll go 'Oh, it's great' and then stop returning my phone calls?"

"Actually, I think I'm incapable of giving false praise. It's, like, a natural deficiency or something."

Ethan squeezed my hand. "Then I'll think about it."

"It's such a nice night," I said, closing my eyes and taking a deep breath. "Hill Pointe really has the best nights."

"Have you ever lived anywhere else?" Ethan asked.

"Not yet."

Ethan jolted a tiny bit. "Are you planning on moving?"

"I don't know. Maybe someday."

"I hope not," Ethan said. "I love it here. My sister is here. My niece and nephews are here. I know this city like the back of my hand."

A huge smile came on my lips as we passed one of my favorite spots—Show Me, the one and only show tune karaoke club in the city. (Loads of tables, a huge grand piano, and a list of all the best songs in the world. Could there be anything better?)

"So then you know where we are?" I asked, smile widening.

"Yep." Ethan walked right past the club, but I stopped, which forced him to stop too.

"Let's go in," I said.

Ethan shook his head. "Nope."

"Come on. I haven't been here in forever."

"I haven't been here in . . . ever."

I tugged on his arm, pulling him toward the door. "Come on, it's prize night. Last time I was here on prize night, I won a brand-new copy of *White Christmas*."

Ethan relented and opened the door for me.

We pushed our way through the crowd inside to an open table. We ordered drinks and settled in.

"I can't believe you've never been here." I looked to the stage where the weekend pianist, Gordon, played as a pretty brunette sang the song "Popular," from *Wicked*.

"That's only because I've never wanted to come." Ethan flashed me a look that let me know he was only mostly serious. "All musicals all the time? No thanks."

I shook my head. "How can you not like musicals?"

"Because I like movies that actually make sense."

"Musicals make sense."

Ethan shifted in his seat, as if getting ready for a serious debate. "What's your favorite musical?"

"*West Side Story*," I answered instantly.

"Makes NO sense!" Ethan gesticulated wildly.

"It's *Romeo and Juliet*!" I argued.

"It's two gangs *dancing* while they fight."

"I can't believe this crazy talk." I pursed my lips. "Next thing you'll tell me you hate *The Sound of Music*."

Ethan closed his eyes like he was in physical pain.

"Are you kidding me? Okay. Well, you have to like *Grease*."

"I have to do no such thing."

I stared at Ethan, mouth agape. "Everyone likes *Grease*."

Ethan picked up his drink. "The only nice thing I can say about *Grease* is that it's not *Grease 2*."

I lifted one shoulder. "I happen to love *Grease 2*."

"Shut. Your. Mouth." Ethan shook his head in exaggerated shock.

"I'm not going to apologize for loving *Grease 2*."

"*Grease 2* should apologize for *Grease 2*!"

"Okay. When was the last time you saw it?"

"I've never seen it!"

I lifted my hands. "How can you judge a movie you haven't even seen?"

"I don't have to watch *Grease 2* to know it's . . . *Grease 2*!"

"Good evening, ladies and gents," Gordon said into the microphone on the piano. "Let's give it up for Brit!"

A load roar came from a table in the corner, filled with twenty-something girls on an obvious girls' night out.

"Up next," Gordon continued, "we have Judy."

Soft claps sounded in the room as a forty-ish woman moved toward the standing microphone. Gordon played a short intro, and then Judy began to sing. It was the song "Fifty Percent," and I got completely sucked into the beauty of it. When the song ended, and I clapped along with everyone, I noticed Ethan staring at my profile.

"Thank you, Judy," Gordon said through the applause. "And now it's time for our Broadway quiz game!"

The room grew loud and excited.

"Do you want to know what we have as tonight's prize?"

The applause intensified.

"Tickets to see . . . *Mary Poppins*! On Broadway!"

The cheers were almost deafening.

"But you can't win unless you play. So get up here!"

A handful of people moved toward the stage, ready for the sudden-death Broadway quiz game that Show Me was famous for.

I popped out of my seat automatically. "Do you mind if I

go up there?" I asked Ethan. "I mean, it's *Mary Poppins*."

He pointed his chin toward the quickly forming line. "Go."

I bent down to hug him and then bounded toward the stage. "Good luck," he called after me.

Ethan's good-luck wishing must've worked, because I killed it up there.

I went onstage four times and got every one of my questions right.

Question 1: *Wicked* took place before what movie?

Question 2: What is the longest running Broadway show in history?

Question 3: Which US President appears as a character in *Annie*?

Question 4: What musical, made into a movie, starred the unlikely duo of Clint Eastwood and Lee Marvin?

Answer Key: *The Wizard of Oz*, *Phantom of the Opera*, Roosevelt, and *Paint Your Wagon*.

But, even better than the fun of answering the questions, was looking out to the crowd and seeing Ethan holding up an American Idol-esque sign he'd made on a bar napkin: Go Jesse!

My heart melted into a little puddle.

And then it was just me and a sweet-looking grandma named Mildred. To the sound of loud cheers, we took our spots onstage. I smiled and offered my hand for her to shake, *Family Feud* style.

She dug her nails into my flesh. "You're going down. You and your frizzy hair."

Whoa. And she looked so nice with her "World's Greatest Grandma" sweatshirt and lavender pants.

"Okay, ladies," Gordon said. "You are the final two contestants!"

The crowd cheered for us.

"As you know, the final round is best out of three. You will have three questions. The first one to get two correct wins the prize!"

More cheering.

"Are you ready?"

"Yes!" I shouted like I was hopped up on way too much sugar.

Then I hovered my hand over the buzzer in front of me, ready to hit it, and gave Mildred my best intimidating look.

"You're gonna lose," she mouthed at me.

"All right," Gordon said. "Here we go. Question one: What musical . . . took place . . . in . . ."

I danced around like I had to use the bathroom.

Gordon squinted, looking down at the card. "What musical took place . . . in . . . Scotland?"

I hit the little buzzer thing so hard it slid across the table.

"Jesse," Gordon said.

"*Brigadoon!*" I yelled in his ear.

"*Brigadoon* is correct," Gordon said with a smile.

Mildred rolled her eyes. "Of course you know the one with a floozy coming onto some guy in a shack in the woods."

"Question two," Gordon said. "If you get this Mildred, you're back in the game. If you get it Jesse, you win."

Mildred eyed me.

"What musical features the song, 'I'm Gonna Wash That Man Right Out of My Hair'?"

I swear I hit the buzzer first.

Like, light years before Mildred. But somehow hers made a sound before mine.

"Mildred," Gordon said.

"*South Pacific.*"

"That's correct."

Mildred did a little shimmy and shot a gloating look at me.

The room grew loud with excited cheers and chatter.

"This is it, ladies," Gordon said. "For the win."

Mildred moved her finger across her neck like a knife.

"What *Peanuts* character does not appear in the musical, *You're a Good Man, Charlie Brown?*"

I moved to slap the buzzer.

But . . . wait. I stopped my hand just above it.

Mildred did the same.

Neither of us knew the answer.

If neither of us wanted to guess, that meant we'd have to go to the next question.

Unless . . .

Suddenly, I moved like I was going to hit the buzzer.

Mildred responded by hitting hers.

The second she realized what had happened, she looked at me in shock.

"Mildred," Gordon said, his voice excited.

"Um . . ." Mildred stammered.

"You have three seconds," Gordon said.

"Um . . . I . . . Snoopy?"

Gordon frowned.

And I knew it was mine.

"I'm sorry, the answer is Woodstock. Jesse! You win!"

The crowd cheered for me as Gordon handed me the envelope containing the two tickets to *Mary Poppins*.

I did not shove the tickets in Mildred's face and say, "Sucka."

I did, however, hold them over my head and run around the room.

When I got back to the table, Ethan gave me a high five, and a bunch of people at surrounding tables congratulated me. I'm not going to lie, I caught myself thinking, I wonder if this is what it's like to be Jimmer Fredette?

I plopped down in my chair and finished off my drink. "Thanks for doing this," I said to Ethan.

He cracked a smile. "It wasn't so bad."

I grabbed the napkin sign he'd made, shoved it into my bag, and stood up. "Okay. We can go now."

Ethan nodded, helped me with my jacket, and walked me to the door with his arm around my shoulders.

We were outside on the sidewalk when he said, "So you sure know your musicals."

"Yeah. I'm kind of a nerd when it comes to that." I chuckled. "You don't love me anymore, do you?"

I completely froze when I realized what I'd said. The word "love" seemed to just sit, suspended in the air between us.

But to my surprise, Ethan stopped walking and looked into my eyes so intently I felt my breath catch. "Actually," he said. "That's the exact opposite of what I was thinking."

I could feel my chest rising and falling quickly, and suddenly the sound of a cab speeding down the waterlogged street came into my ears. Instantly, Ethan picked me up and moved me out of the path of the impending puddle splash.

I squealed at the movement, and then cringed as Ethan took the brunt of the water.

"Oh no," I said as he set me down.

But Ethan just kept his eyes on me, like all he'd wanted was to protect me.

I took a couple breaths, trying to slow my fast heartbeat.

But it sped up more as Ethan brushed my hair out of my face. I felt heat rise up in every place his fingers touched. I closed my eyes and leaned in toward him. A few thick, heavy seconds later, our lips met like it was what they were made to do. The whole world turned to blurry light and sound.

And in that moment, I knew my life was going to be measured in terms of the moments leading up to the kiss and the moments after it.

thirteen

"Hello. Is this Jesse Young?"

"Yes. This is . . . me . . . she."

"Hi, Miss Young. My name is Claire Overton, and I'm the director of Alive Academy of the Arts."

"Yes. Of course." I smiled excitedly at Laurel, who was sitting across the table, picking at a Sugar House Coffee vegan chocolate muffin.

"Who is it?" she mouthed.

"The art job lady," I mouthed back.

Laurel flashed me a thumbs-up.

"I'm calling to see if you're still interested in working for us," Claire said.

"Absolutely!"

"Great." I heard the rustling of papers. "I'm in Austin right now, but I would like to interview you before I leave. Would you be available for a telephone interview a week from today, at 9:00 a.m. eastern?"

"Yes. I would be honored!"

"Wonderful," Claire said. "We will give you a call next Saturday at 9:00."

"I'll be waiting for your call." *Okay. This is where you wow her with your art knowledge.* "As long as my clocks don't melt in Dali-esque fashion."

Awkward pause. "I'll talk to you in a week."

"I'm looking forward to it." I hung up and stared at the phone in my hand.

"I knew you were going to get it," Laurel said.

I couldn't help but do a little happy dance in my seat. "This is so exciting. Thank you so much for passing on the job info."

Laurel smiled. "That's what cousins do."

I nodded. "So, as I was saying, how's Clint?"

Laurel sighed. "He's fine. But I don't know how much longer I can pretend to care about whales, trees, and the ozone layer. It's costing me a fortune."

I couldn't help but laugh.

"And, as I was saying," Laurel wiggled her eyebrows excitedly, "I know something you don't know."

I leaned forward with interest. "What?"

Laurel took a sip of her cinnamon tea and smiled into her mug. "Someone is taking you to the Poconos today."

I practically jumped out of my seat. "The Poconos! Are you serious?"

Laurel nodded. "To the Bloom Hotel and Spa."

"No way!" I suddenly felt a surge of happiness, kind of like you get after you eat a lot of chocolate.

I love The Poconos. Like, crazy, dreamy love. It was late March, but it had been a long winter, so the mountains were still snowy and magical.

And though I wasn't exactly sure, I had a hunch as to who was taking me. And the thought made my heart beat a little faster.

"How do you know about this?" I asked Laurel.

"Because he called and asked me if you'd rather have a wrap, a salt scrub, or a massage."

"He who?" I asked quickly.

Laurel shook her head. "Nope. I think it's sweet that he wants to surprise you."

"So what treatment did you tell him I'd like best?"

"Massage, of course."

I nodded. "That's my girl."

More chocolate-y happiness swirled through me. I love massages almost as much as I love The Poconos. There's a lady who comes into Sugar House twice a month and does chair massages in fifteen-minute increments. I get in that chair and I just hand her twenty after twenty in my dazed state.

"So," Laurel set her mug down, "now onto why I'm really here."

"That wasn't why you're here?"

"Not the whole reason."

I braced myself. "Okay . . ."

"Bloom Hotel and Spa has arguably the best spa in the state. In fact, it was rated in *The Hill Pointe Free Press* as most likely to be visited by Kate Middleton."

I rolled my eyes. Laurel is obsessed with Kate Middleton. She has a "Kate's Greats" board in her bedroom, filled with photos of Kate's best fashion moments. And Laurel was one of the lucky few who got on net-a-porter.com in time to order the blue Issa dress Kate wore when she and William announced their engagement.

"All right . . ." I said, eyes on my cousin.

"You girls want some more tea?" Magda asked as she appeared at the side of the table, teapot in hand.

Laurel nodded and pushed her cup to the edge.

"What's the dish?" Magda asked as she poured the tea.

"Jesse's going to the mountains with a boy," Laurel said proudly.

Magda met my eye. "Don't you dare wear that puffer coat of yours. It makes you look like a stack of tires. It's all about layers."

"Got it."

As my boss walked away, Laurel reached around and grabbed her Fendi handbag from the back of the chair. She dug in it for a minute and produced a large piece of paper. She smoothed it out on the table, and I quickly realized it was a map. On the top were the words, "Bloom Hotel and Spa."

Uh-oh.

"This is a map of Bloom Hotel and Spa." Laurel's voice was all business. "Your mission is simple: Get me three things."

"What are you talking about?"

"You will enter the spa here." Laurel used a coffee stirrer to point to a spot on the map marked Point of Origin. "You'll be greeted at the front desk. You'll enjoy a glass of cucumber water. And then you will do whatever you need to do to get into this bathroom." She pointed to another spot on the map.

"Because?"

"Products," Laurel said simply. "Samples of everything from Peter Thomas Roth body wash to Frederic Fekkai shampoo to Philosophy face cream. They're for people who forgot to bring something. You will pretend you forgot everything. And you will place all of the products in this bag." Laurel handed me a black bag.

I half expected it to have a dollar sign on it.

"Laur—"

She cut me off. "Next you will be taken to a dressing room to prepare for your massage. In this dressing room, you will find a plush robe and a pair of slippers. These are made in France and not sold online. You will shove the robe and slippers into this tote and pretend you never saw them." Laurel set a collapsible tote on the table.

"What? I can't do that. I—"

Laurel hit the map. "Are you with me or not soldier?!"

I stared at her, blinking.

"They'll just charge your credit card," she said. "I'll pay you back."

I let my shoulders sink down. "Okay. What's the last thing?"

Laurel took a slow sip of her tea. "Mud."

"Mud," I repeated.

"Yes. This," Laurel pointed to a little triangle on the map, "is The Mud Hut. You will do whatever it takes to get out there. *Whatever* it takes. And you will fill this jar with mud."

"Um . . ." I scratched my head as Laurel set a jar on the table. "Can't you just . . . go out to your backyard and get some mud there?"

Laurel looked at me like I'd just asked her to brush her teeth with toilet water. "The mud at Bloom is made from volcanic ash imported from Calistoga, California."

I looked at the jar. Then at my crazy cousin. "Laurel, you know I love you. But all of this sounds a little . . ."

Before I could finish, she set something else on the table.

I immediately froze.

There, in front of me, was an original copy of *The Sound of Music* soundtrack, signed by Julie Andrews. It was the most beautiful thing I'd ever seen. I reached for it and could actually hear the sound of my heart beating in my ears.

But Laurel quickly pulled the album out of my reach. "You get me what I want," she said. "And you'll get what you want."

Without a word, I shoved the black sack, tote, jar, and map into my bag.

fourteen

"Cucumber water, Miss?"

I smiled as the pretty spa receptionist handed me a glass. "Thank you."

As I sipped the refreshing drink, I snuck a look at Troy, who was next to me, checking us in for our treatments. He looked so good in his jeans and cashmere sweater, his chin all scruffy and yum.

I noticed the receptionist staring at him too, and when I caught her, she pretended to be looking at a bowl of oranges on the desk.

"Okay." Troy set the spa's pen down on the desk and turned to me. "We're all set."

"Thank you so, so much for bringing me here," I said, my eyes wandering to the plush furniture, roaring fireplace, and expansive view of the breathtaking snow-covered mountains.

"Did you decide what to call our holiday yet?" Troy asked.

I scrunched up my lips, thinking of the text he'd sent in the morning.

Today is Make Up Your Own Holiday Day. Let's celebrate. I'll be at your place in an hour. Bring a coat, gloves, and scarf. Can't wait.

"I'm still thinking," I said.

Troy nodded. "A girl who likes to take her time."

His words hit something in me. I usually was the girl who liked to take her time. But Troy brought out a more free-spirited side of me, and I was really enjoying it.

"Are you two ready for your treatments?" the receptionist asked.

I took one last sip of my water, trying to soak up every last bit of calm. As soon as that water was gone, my mission was going to begin.

"Actually," I said as I set the glass down. "I think I'm going to run to the restroom."

"Of course," the girl said. "It's just down the hall to your right."

"Thanks." I turned to Troy. "I'll be right back."

Troy slipped an arm around my waist for a wonderful moment. "I'll be here."

My heart sped up as I moved down the hall, past the bathroom the receptionist had referred to, and on to the one attached to the steam room. I held my breath as I swung the door open and honed in on the baskets of samples on the marble counter.

The room was completely empty, and I breathed a sigh of relief. Maybe this wasn't going to be so bad after all.

I quickly retrieved the black bag from Laurel's tote. But just as I did, a trio of perfectly coiffed women with towels wrapped around their bodies emerged from the steam room door and looked over at me. The diamonds on their left hands were as big as golf balls.

I made a big show of looking in the black bag. "Oh, dear!" I gasped. "I forgot my toiletry case!"

The women retrieved their belongings from their lockers and began primping, whispering to each other.

"I guess my driver forgot to put it in the Range Rover," I continued, shaking my head. "Oh, well. I guess this stuff will work since I'm in a pinch."

And with that I dropped some Jo Malone body cream into Laurel's bag.

And a few bars of Peter Thomas Roth soap.

And a bottle of Alterna shampoo.

And a whole set of Philosophy products.

I'd never heard of any of the stuff. Which probably meant it was good. Laurel is pretty much horrified when she sees my 3-in-1 shampoo, body wash, and car cleaner.

The women pretended not to watch me, but I could practically feel their judgment.

"Ta, ladies!" I said as I strolled toward the door and pushed it open with a flourish.

Outside, I let the door close behind me, rested my back against it, and hugged the goods to my chest.

One task down. Two to go.

I headed back to the spa entrance where I found Troy sitting on a fluffy white couch, reading a fishing magazine.

I came up behind him and bent down, resting my arms on the back of the couch. "Hey."

Troy shut his magazine and looked back at me. "All set?"

I nodded.

Troy stood and grabbed my hand in his take-charge, don't-wait-for-permission way. We walked, hand in hand, back to the reception desk, where we were directed to our respective locker rooms.

"See you soon," I said over my shoulder as we parted in opposite directions.

The look in Troy's eye sent a surge though my body. "Can't wait," he said.

After a short walk, I reached the women's locker room.

My massage therapist greeted me immediately with the shake of her soft yet strong hand. "Hello. My name is Bea, and I am looking forward to working with you. Have you been to Bloom Spa before?"

I shook my head.

Bea had me fill out some paperwork and then showed me to a dressing room. She moved the cream satin curtain back and took a quick look inside. Her eyes settled on the robe and slippers perched on the smooth wooden bench. As soon as I saw them, my heart rate sped up.

I would never make it as a professional thief.

"I'll wait outside while you change," Bea said. "Call me if you need anything."

"Okay. Thanks."

I stood inside the dressing room for a minute, trying to figure out what to do. Bea had looked right at the robe and slippers. It wasn't like I could just tell her they weren't there. But . . . *The Sound of Music* . . .

After another moment of deliberation, I took a deep breath, shoved the robe and slippers into Laurel's tote, and called out, "Bea?"

"Do you need something?" she asked.

"Yes. You said there was a robe and slippers in here, but I don't see them."

Technically it wasn't a lie.

"Are you sure?" Bea asked.

"Yes," I squeaked.

Again, technically it was true.

Bea came into the dressing room and looked around, her brow deeply furrowed. For a split second, I swear she wanted to ask me to open the tote and show her what was inside.

But finally she just said, "I'll get you some."

I smiled in relief and sat down on the bench.

And then Bea came back. In her hand was a crumpled up robe with what I really, really hope were spray-tan marks on it, and a wet pair of slippers. She'd obviously gotten them out of a dirty clothing pile somewhere. She held them out, her face challenging me to take them or fess up about the ones I obviously had in my bag.

I repeated *The Sound of Music* in my mind over and over as

I put on the robe and slippers. Then I followed Bea to a gorgeous massage room. And as I slipped under the soft sheet on the massage table, and Bea worked my weary muscles, I forgot everything.

The robe and slippers.

All of the stress in my life.

My name.

I showered, put on a clean robe I found in the locker room, and was about to change back into my clothes when I heard something that instantly caught my attention. It was a group of young women, dressed in pink silk dressing gowns. One of them had a veil on her head, and I quickly surmised they were members of a bridal party.

"Okay, girls!" a tall brunette said. "Time to go to The Mud Hut!"

The girls all squealed and headed for the door.

I quickly grabbed the jar from my locker and shoved it into my pocket. And, without thinking, I joined the group, following them trough the heated outdoor corridor that led to The Mud Hut. Once there, the girls stood in front of the entrance, giggling and talking. The spa worker guarding the door eyed me suspiciously.

So I giggled along with the group and said, "So . . . that best man is one hot number, isn't he?"

The worker let the group, including me, into the hut—which was kind of gross, but also kind of cool, with its huge pool of, well, mud. The girls stripped down to their swimsuits, stepped into the pool, and commented on how strange it felt.

I put my hand in. "Yeah. That's weird."

"Um." The bride frowned at me. "We have The Mud Hut for the next hour. Private reservation."

"Oh. I'm not getting in. I'm just here to . . ." *Okay. Think of something.* Quick. " . . . take a sample." And with that, I pulled the jar out of my pocket.

The group got suddenly quiet, and all eyes were on me.

The bride crossed her arms. "What?"

"Do you want me to go talk to the guy outside?" the brunette asked her.

"No!" I said quickly. "I'm with the . . ." I lowered my voice to a whisper. "Mud Bath Quality Association. If they know I'm here they might . . . make adjustments."

The girls stared at me, suddenly rapt.

"And you don't want them to be able to hide anything." I quickly scooped some mud into the jar in a scientific fashion. "I went to a place down the road last month. The mud was proven to be from a farm in . . . North Dakota."

The girls gasped.

I nodded as I continued to scoop. "I know."

"So will you post the findings online or something?" a girl whose curly hair was in a messy ponytail asked.

I tightened the lid on the jar. "What?"

"The results of the test. How do we know if the mud passes?" Uh . . .

"If you don't hear anything, the mud is good," I said.

"Where do we go to check?" the brunette asked.

"Our website is . . . um . . . www.AllMudIsNotEqual.web." The girls nodded.

"Okay." I patted the jar of mud. "I'm off to the lab."

The mud bathers bid me good-bye, and I booked it out of the hut and back to the locker room.

I quickly dressed, brushed my hair, and put some gloss on my lips. When I emerged, Troy was waiting down the hall, looking all relaxed and refreshed, holding a wrapped gift.

"There you are." His eyes crinkled at the corners. "How was your massage?"

"Amazing." I let out a breath. "This is all . . . so amazing."

"That's what I was going for." Troy handed me the package.

I lifted my eyebrows and ripped into the shiny paper. Inside I found . . . "Scrabble!"

Troy leaned against the wall behind him, looking satisfied.

"Are we going to play?" I asked hopefully.

Troy nodded. "Of course. By the fire. I had the restaurant reserve us a table."

I threw my arms around his neck and inhaled the scent of his freshly showered skin. "I can't believe you remembered."

"I don't really have a choice." Troy breathed into my hair. "You occupy a good many of my thoughts."

My skin got all tingly, like I'd just slathered on a bunch of peppermint lotion. "Play Scrabble by the Fire Day," I said, my mouth in a wide grin.

Troy nodded. "I like it."

A little while later, we were at a table by the fire in the hotel's five-star restaurant. I'd just finished the most amazing eggplant parmesan I'd ever eaten, Troy and I were sharing a piece of cheesecake, and I was one word away from beating him at Scrabble.

Though I'm ninety-nine percent sure he was letting me win.

I drew my tiles—loving the clicking sound they made as they hit against each other in the box—and smiled when I got the one letter I needed to spell my word: Spontaneous.

I set down my tiles and shot Troy a look of victory.

And just like that, he stood up, pulled out my chair, and helped me put on my coat and scarf. "Well, Scrabble Champ," he said, "fittingly, I have another surprise for you."

"What about . . . ?" I eyed the game on the table.

"The busboy knows what to do," Troy said simply.

My face warm with anticipation, I followed Troy out of the restaurant and to a hidden staircase that reminded me of something out of a storybook. After climbing the stairs, we exited a creaky door and were on the roof of the hotel.

I took a second to take it all in. The view of the snow-topped mountains. The crisp, cold air and the way it felt in my lungs, against my face. The bright, vivid stars that dotted the sky. Being with a man who helped me live so much in the moment.

"Wow," I said, pulling my coat tight around me. "How did you get them to let you up here?"

"Secrets are a key part of any relationship." Troy put his arms around me, warming me instantly. "Wouldn't you agree?"

I released a breath, noticing I could see the warm air as it hit the cold. "You have no idea."

"This is the best place around to see the stars," Troy said.

I looked up at the clear sky. "It's incredible."

"You're incredible." Troy suddenly got very still, and I could almost feel a change in the air. "Really. I've never met anyone like you. I really like you, Jesse."

I leaned back into Troy. "I really like you."

Troy gently spun me around, so I was facing him. "I mean I think I'm falling for you," he said.

And before I knew what was happening, Troy was cradling my face with his hands. His warm skin on my cold cheeks sent the most amazing sensation through my entire body. After a second, his lips met mine and he kissed me with such intensity, I leaned against him to keep from losing my footing. The whole thing took me by complete surprise, and that made it so much better. No time to think. No time to analyze.

Breathless, with my lips still next to his, I whispered, "Kiss Under the Stars Day."

Troy nodded in approval.

And then he kissed me again.

···→ ◆ ←···

David was waiting up for me when I got home.

He always does.

One of the many, many reasons I love him.

Laurel was there too—though probably for more selfish reasons. The second I came through the door, she bounced up. I handed over what she was obviously waiting for, and she squeezed me until it was hard for me to breathe.

"Thank you! Thank you! Thank you!"

I smiled and moved into the living room, where I sat on the floor in front of the chair Laurel had been sitting in.

David was on the couch, a bowl of popcorn in his lap. "Good date?"

"Yeah!" Laurel called over her shoulder as she examined her goodies. "Dish."

I stared off into the distance. "It was . . . great."

David fixed me with a stare.

"What?" I asked.

But I knew what. David thought I was fooling myself with this running around dating thing.

"It just sounds like it's getting serious," he said.

"Leave her alone." Laurel threw an empty lotion box at him as she came into the living room and sat down behind me. "Get back to your I'm-never-going-to-have-a-girlfriend Saturday night movie."

"I don't know what I'm doing anymore." I leaned back into Laurel's knees, and she massaged my head. "I'm just . . . I'm thinking about Ethan. I mean, he's made it totally clear that we can take things as slow as I want to. That I don't need to tell him anything until I'm ready. But still . . ."

"You're overthinking it," Laurel said.

I closed my eyes. "I just have to figure out . . . how I'm going to figure this out."

"And you will," Laurel said. "You're not in a normal sitch, hon. You have to face that."

"I know."

Laurel rubbed my temples. "Do you remember when we were in tenth grade, and I really wanted to make the cheer squad, and you thought it was the dumbest thing ever because you were all Miss Tortured Artist with those freaky pictures in your locker?"

"Yeah," I said, not knowing what this had to do with anything.

"And remember how you told me to do a dance to Tripping Daisies."

I smiled. "I knew everyone else would be doing TLC and Coolio songs, and you needed to stand out."

"And you were right," Laurel said. "You may be my little cousin, but you always know what to do."

"You really think that?"

"I really do."

"And you think I'll be happy like . . . happy-with-a-guy happy?"

Laurel reached down and hugged me before hopping up and heading into the kitchen. "I know you will."

I looked over at my brother. "You're a guy—"

Laurel snorted loudly.

"—What would you want a girl to do if she was—"

David looked at me with the sweet concern of a brother. "Just lay it all out there. Tell Ethan everything."

I made a pained expression. "Am I making a mess?"

"No." David frowned. "Maybe. I don't know."

I took a sharp inhale of breath and got up from the floor. "I'm going to tell Ethan everything. The next time I see him." I moved toward the kitchen. "And if he leaves me, then . . . problem solved, right? I mean, if he doesn't think I'm worth it—"

"Then he's an idiot," David said like only a brother can.

"I agree with the dwarf," Laurel said through a mouthful of chocolate ice cream.

fifteen

My stomach was in big, fat knots.

I stared out the window as Ethan and I drove a little out of the city, leaving behind the row homes and office buildings, and seeing in their place trees and stately homes with large yards.

"Are you all right?" Ethan asked, sensing my anxiety.

I looked over at him, heart pounding. "I have to tell you something."

"Okay." Ethan reached across the gearshift and grabbed my hand. His touch was comforting in the most excruciating way.

"But not now," I said quickly. "After the barbecue."

"Okay," Ethan said simply.

"Okay," I said with a nod of finality.

As Ethan flicked on his turn signal and pulled into the driveway of a lovely colonial, I told myself to put the impending conversation out of my mind, to enjoy this time with Ethan.

After all, who knew if it would be the last time he ever wanted to talk to me.

We exited the car and walked up the front steps, and with my hand in Ethan's, I felt myself begin to relax. I smiled over at him as he reached out to knock on the door.

But then he suddenly stopped and looked over at me. "Listen, I have to warn you."

My throat got tight.

I mean, has anyone you know ever started a sentence with, "Listen, I have to warn you," and then finished it with something good?

Like: Listen, I have to warn you, I just found fifty thousand dollars, and I want to give it to you!

Or: Listen, I have to warn you, Julie Andrews wrote a book and she's in town signing copies!

Or: Listen, I have to warn you, John Lennon really is alive and living in London, and I just bought you an airline ticket to the other side of the pond.

No.

It's always something bad.

Like: My family saw a picture of you, and they think you're kind of a dog.

Or: My sister and her husband are in a cult, so they might ask you to give them a hundred bucks tonight. And you probably should.

"Yeah?" I asked, fixing my eyes on Ethan.

"My sister's house can be a little . . ." Ethan paused, searching for the right word. "Intense."

I let out a long sigh of relief and squeezed his hand.

I could handle intense.

No sooner did I have this thought than the front door suddenly swung open and dozens of pea-sized, black things began to fly out, pelting me and Ethan.

I quickly hid behind him, using his body as a shield. One of the things hit me in the shoulder and fell to the ground by my foot. I picked it up.

What the heck? Is that a black bean?

"Ah!" Ethan cried as he shielded me. "We surrender!"

"Say the magic word!" Our attacker—a pint-sized boy dressed in head-to-toe camouflage and a Spiderman mask—cried out.

"Samurai Warrior!" Ethan tried. "Abominable Snowman!"

A pink-clad girl holding a Barbie in each hand, rushed to the rescue and whispered to me, "It's Super Ninja."

"Thanks." With a wink at the girl, I whispered the words to Ethan.

"Super Ninja!" Ethan shouted as he grabbed the little boy and slung him over his shoulder.

"Nope! That's not it!" The boy slid down Ethan's back and started to karate kick his legs.

"Guys," Ethan looked at the kids with a sweet love, "this is Jesse."

The kids gave me the kid-over to see if I looked like I was any fun.

I suddenly wished I'd practiced a magic trick or something. But then again, the last time I tried to impress kids with a "magic trick," I decided to show them my double-jointed shoulders, and they ran away screaming.

"Hi!" I said.

Ethan touched their little heads one by one. "This is Conner and Hayley."

Hayley grinned at me. "You're pretty."

"No." I touched her nose. "You're pretty."

"No, she's not! She looks like a toilet!" Connor laughed really loud and began trying to pull off Ethan's shoes. "Uncle Ethan, I think we can play with the lightsabers today. Mom took them out of time out."

"Nu-uh, Conner," Hayley said. "You got them taken away again for jumping off the refrigerator."

"Did not, Hayley!" Conner argued.

"Did too!"

"Okay!" A pretty, exhausted-looking woman with a baby monitor clipped to her jeans came into the room. "Why don't you guys go play in the living room?"

The kids reluctantly scampered off, but not before Conner made a face behind his mother's back.

The woman hugged Ethan. "Hey, Big E."

"This is my sister, Sarah," Ethan said to me.

I smiled, so happy to know another part of Ethan's life. "Hi. It's nice to meet you."

Sarah grinned back. "So good to meet you. Welcome to the circus." A scream came from the baby monitor. "That's Adam, our littlest."

"Oh. Bill," Ethan jutted his chin as a guy came into the house via the back door, "this is Jesse."

We walked over to meet the man, who was holding a spatula and wearing an apron that said, "Keeper of the Flame."

He reached out and shook my hand. "Hi, Jesse. Bill Walters."

I smiled warmly. "Hi."

"As you can see." Sarah put her hands in the air. "We keep it pretty informal around here. So please, make yourself comfortable. Dinner is almost ready."

Bill regarded me. "We've got some serious barbecue going on out back. But Ethan told us you're a vegetarian, so don't worry, I got you some pork."

"Great . . ."

Ethan put an arm around me and smiled. "The other . . . not meat."

⋯⟶ ◆ ⟵⋯

"This food is delicious." I took a bite of potato salad and leaned back in the patio chair, peering over at adorable little Adam, sleeping away in his portable crib. "Thank you again for having me over."

Sarah moved her gaze away from Conner and Hayley, who were playing on a swing set on the lawn, and focused on me. "Thank you for coming."

"Hello! Is anyone home?"

Brow furrowed, I looked to the gate, where none other than Maddy was standing with a plate of cookies in her hand.

"Come on in," Sarah said.

Maddy approached the table and set down the cookies. "Hi, Ethan," she said sweetly. Then she fixed her eyes on me. "Leslie."

"Actually it's Jesse."

Maddy sat down in the empty chair next to Ethan. "I like your shirt."

Ethan looked down at his plaid button down. "Thanks."

"I'm so glad you're here," Maddy continued. "I'm having trouble with an article I'm working on for the school paper. And I thought, who better to help me than a real-live newspaper guy?"

"Okay." Ethan scratched his head. "I guess I could help."

"Great." Maddy took her phone out of her pocket. "The article is about what our locker decorations say about us."

Ethan played with his red plastic cup. "Cool."

Maddy's cheeks turned pink. "Really? You think so?"

"I still remember what I had in my locker when I was younger," I offered.

Maddy shot me a look that was pure hatred. "Well, now you're old."

"So what questions do you have?" Ethan asked quickly.

"Well," Maddy consulted her phone, "let's see. Would you rather have a picture of an animal, a band, or a girl in your locker?"

Ethan thought for a second. "Probably a band."

Maddy nodded. "Okay . . . but if you did have a picture of a girl, what would she look like?"

"Well . . ." The right corner of Ethan's mouth turned up, and for a split second he looked over at me.

"Forget that question," Maddy said instantly. "Why don't you tell me what bands you like?"

Ethan leaned back in his seat. "The Killers. The White Stripes. Death Cab for Cutie."

"I love Death Cab!" I said, looking over at him.

"I wish I could put you in a death cab," Maddy said under her breath.

I frowned. "What?"

"Why aren't you eating a hot dog?" Maddy asked slowly, as if she were repeating her words.

"Because—"

Maddy cut me off. "I mean, you came here for a barbecue. Don't you think it's a little rude not to eat the food?" She shot Sarah a look that said, "I'm so sorry Ethan picked such a loser."

"Actually, I'm a vegetarian."

Maddy made a pitiful face. "Is that because you don't want to get fatter?"

Not fat. Fatter.

"No," I said. "It's because I think it's good for the environment and for your health."

"If it's good for your health, then how come your hair is always so, well, you know . . . ?" She eyed my hair with contempt.

"Hey, Maddy!" Sarah said. "Could you pass me the ketchup?"

Maddy nodded and passed down the bottle. "Thanks for the help, Ethan," she said in a syrupy voice. "I also wanted to tell you I started writing a play. You were my inspirashe."

Ethan nodded. "That's great, Maddy."

"What are you writing these days?" she asked him, fluttering her lashes.

"I started something new, actually." Ethan took hold of my hand, and a warmth filled my chest.

Maddy watched, her fingers tightening around the plastic knife in her hand. "Do you write, Jesse?"

"Nope."

"Jesse's an artist," Ethan said, beaming at me.

"That's too bad," Maddy said. "I read this article in a magazine, and it said that couples should have things in common. Or else they're doomed to break up. Usually within a few months. Maybe even days."

"Madeleine Renee!"

All eyes went to the gate, where a very angry-looking woman stood.

"You're supposed to be in your room studying. Not making a mess of my kitchen and leaving the oven on."

"Mom," Maddy grumbled, her cheeks flushing with embarrassment.

"Get back to the house," the woman said.

Head down, Maddy rushed to the gate.

"Sorry about that," the woman said to Sarah.

"Always an adventure at the Walters house," Bill said as Maddy and her mom walked off.

As if on cue, Conner came bounding up to the table. "Come on, Uncle Ethan," he said. "Let's play Ninja Tag."

Ethan rustled the boy's hair. "I think we're going to relax for a few minutes."

"Come on," Connor said. "Pleeeeeeeease."

My heart swelled at the sight of his adorable face. "How can you say no to that?"

Ethan hopped up. "Okay. I won't be gone long. I'm really good at this game."

I watched with a huge smile, as Ethan ran around the yard, pretending to wield a sword. "He really is good at this game," I said, turning to Bill and Sarah.

"He should be." Bill took a sip of his drink. "He's had enough practice."

"Your kids are beautiful."

"Thank you," Sarah said. "They sure love their uncle."

After a moment, Hayley came up and sat in Ethan's vacated seat. She fixed her sweet little eyes on mine. "Are you and Ethan going to get married and have a baby?"

"Okay!" Sarah said, pulling an apologetic face. "Hayley, I think Uncle Ethan needs to be chased!"

I took a deep breath and blinked, staring at the precious little girl as she ran back out to the yard to play with the boys. I wiped at my eyes, feeling tears threaten.

"You okay?" Sarah asked.

"Fine," I said quickly. "It's just my crazy allergies."

···→ ◆ ←···

"Bye!" Ethan and I waved one last time from beside the car and watched as the front door closed.

Ethan massaged his shoulder. "Seriously. I think I hurt something."

I smiled. "Those kids are so crazy about you, 'Big E.'"

"Well, I'm crazy about them."

Ethan opened my door for me, and I stared at the house as he got into the driver's seat.

"Oh." Ethan stopped in the middle of putting his seatbelt on and looked over at me. "I almost forgot. I found something of yours."

"What?"

Ethan let the seatbelt retract and reached into the back seat. "Close your eyes."

I stared at him suspiciously.

"Close."

I snapped my lids shut.

"Okay . . . and . . . open!"

I opened my eyes and could not believe what I saw.

"Firefly!" I shouted, quickly grabbing the gorgeous My Little Pony from Ethan's hands. I touched her blue mane. I traced the lightning bolts on her side. I inhaled her pungent vinyl smell, suddenly met with a flood of memories. My long-lost friend, back in my hands again. "But . . . how did you . . . ? Where did you . . . ?"

"She just showed up on my doorstep yesterday," Ethan said matter-of-factly. Then he cracked a smile. "In a box marked eBay."

Ethan was grinning from ear to ear. He was just so happy to make me happy. I could hardly contain my glee as I threw my arms around him and squeezed like I'd never let go.

"This is the nicest thing anyone has ever done for me," I said, my voice filled with emotion.

Ethan pulled away, his brow furrowed. "Oh, come on. I hope that's not true."

I wrapped my arms around him again, kissing his cheek. "Thank you," I whispered.

"You are so welcome." Ethan put the key in the ignition but stopped short of starting the engine. "Oh yeah. What did you want to tell me?"

I looked over at him. "What?"

"On our way here, you told me there was something you wanted to tell me."

My heart sunk as the warmth of the moment suddenly left, leaving a cold, hard rock in the bottom of my stomach.

"Oh . . . right . . ." I sat up straighter in my seat, as if to brace myself. I took a deep breath. And another.

But when I looked over at Ethan, I couldn't do it.

I just couldn't.

"I . . ." I looked down at Firefly. "I wanted to tell you how happy you make me."

"Good. I like you happy." Ethan cocked his head to the side. "Was that it?"

I nodded, holding my breath for some reason. "Yeah."

"You know you can talk to me about anything, right?"

"I know," I said too chirpily.

"I'll prove it," Ethan said with a warm, open look. "Talk to me right now."

"Really. There's nothing."

"Okay," Ethan said. But his tone said he didn't believe me. He started the car, and we drove away from the house in silence.

I stared out the window, hoping he didn't see the tear that slid down my cheek.

sixteen

I'm a chicken.

A coward.

A yella-bellied, lily-livered whatever.

And it was all I could think about as I sat on my living room couch the next morning.

Which wasn't good.

Because I really needed to think positive things about myself at that moment.

Like, that very moment.

"So, Miss Young. Tell me your greatest strengths."

I stared at a yellow pencil on the coffee table. "Well, I . . ." Nothing was coming. "I . . . I'm pretty good at hailing a cab."

"Anything else?"

"Not that I can think of."

"All right then. Tell me your greatest weaknesses."

I rolled the pencil off the table. "I'm a liar. I'm a coward. And sometimes I have absolutely no idea what I'm doing."

"Well, Miss Young. In light of what you just told me, I think you're perfect for this job."

"Really?"

"No! Of course not! You can't tell them something like that!"

I sighed. "I know."

I guess it was good I was doing this practice interview with Laurel.

She coughed into the phone. "Come on, Jesse. Are you going to focus? Because otherwise, I'm going back to bed."

I leaned back and rested my head on a throw pillow. "Don't go back to bed. I need you."

"That's for sure."

I closed my eyes. I'm not going to lie. The first thing I saw was Ethan, in that car, holding Firefly. I forced the image out of my mind and replaced it with a block of cheese.

I don't know. It was the first thing that came to my mind.

"Okay," Laurel said. "Let's go over the question about your strengths. You have to come up with something. Preferably something that has to do with the job. Since this is a teaching position, you could say something like, 'I enjoy working with children. I believe children are our future. I enjoy shaping young minds.'"

I wrote down what Laurel said word for word. "Got it."

"Now onto the question about your weaknesses. You want to make sure anything you say has nothing to do with your ability to perform the job. Like you can say you don't know anything about . . . fishing."

"Okay."

"Or the ever-popular spin-it-into-something-good technique: 'I tend to be a perfectionist. I work too hard. I stubbornly stick to my ideals no matter what.'"

That was good. I wrote it down. "Okay. Got it."

"I can't believe you're so clueless about job interviews," Laurel said. "How have you ever gotten a job?"

I thought for a moment. "I guess I've never really had a formal job interview. I worked for the radio station all through college and then after I graduated. And since then, I've gotten jobs from people I know, or people who want to 'help' me."

"Well then, you're lucky," Laurel said. "Now. I know you

tend to blurt things out when you're talking to anyone you perceive to be an authority."

Not that again.

"You say that. But I bet you can't think of another example."

Laurel cleared her throat. "Telling the cop who pulled you over for rolling a stop sign that you once took a magazine from the doctor's office and that you sometimes download songs off the Internet. Telling the dorm janitor who asked you if you knew who left their backpack by the vending machines that you sometimes put regular trash in the recycle-only cans. Telling—"

"Okay. So you have more than one."

"I'm just saying, be selective. Only say things you'd want to see said about yourself on TMZ."

"Got it."

Brrrring. Brrrring. The house phone blared.

"That's them," I said.

"You're going to be great."

"You think so?"

"No idea."

I quickly hung up my cell, took a long, deep breath, and picked the cordless up off the coffee table. "Hello," I said, my voice suddenly shaking with nerves.

"Hello. Is this Jesse?"

"Yes, it is."

"Well, good morning, Jesse. This is Claire Overton. I am joined with two of my colleagues here in Austin. Kerry White and Taylor Newton."

"Hello. Ms. White. Mr. Newton."

"Call me Kerry," a male voice said.

"And me Taylor," a female one put in.

Oops. Wrong gender on both.

"Okay," I said.

"So, Jesse," Claire said in an airy voice. "Before we proceed, I wanted to ask you something. On your application you indicated that you were interested in working in Hill Pointe."

Every bit of me was sweating. Even my earlobes. "That's right."

"Would you be willing to work at one of our other locations?"

Hmm. I hadn't thought about that. I wasn't even sure where all of the other locations were. I remembered seeing Portland on the list. And Brooklyn. And Austin, Texas . . . I think.

"Jesse? Are you still there?"

"Yes." Boy was my voice shaky. "Well . . . Hill Pointe is obviously my first choice, but, yes, I suppose I'd be willing."

"Excellent," Claire said. "Then let's proceed."

I frowned. *Then* let's proceed? As in, had I said no, they would have hung up on me?

"I was very impressed with your resume and your portfolio, Jesse," Taylor said.

"As was I," Kerry added. "I particularly related to the piece called, 'I wish I would have sold his Dale Murphy–signed baseball when that guy offered me a thousand bucks for it.' It was moving, poignant."

Ah yes, one of Darla's favorites as well.

Apparently, Earth-shattering heartbreak is bad for the heart, the mind, and the soul.

But it's great for art.

"You're a talented young artist," Claire said.

The words put a smile on my face. The first one to appear there in hours.

"Since we agree about your art," Claire continued. "This interview is mostly to help us determine if you are a fit for our academy."

"Of course."

"Great," Claire said. "First off, Jesse, what would you say are your three biggest strengths?"

Wow. Laurel called it.

I gulped and looked down at the paper on the coffee table. "I love working with children. I believe they are our future. I enjoy shaping young minds."

"Go on . . ." Claire said.

Go on? But my list was empty.

"Well . . . When I say I enjoy shaping young minds, I mean really molding them. Taking them into my hands and squishing them . . . like Play Doh."

"I see," Claire said.

"Interesting," Kerry put in.

"Could you list your three biggest weaknesses?" Claire asked.

I consulted my notes again. Make your weaknesses sound like good things, i.e. I work too hard.

"I like paint a little too much," I said.

"Are you saying . . ." Claire's voice sounded concerned. "You have some kind of problem?"

Problem? What?

"No! No. I don't mean like, I'm a . . ." I lowered my voice to a whisper. " . . . huffer."

"That's exactly what a huffer would say," I heard Taylor whisper.

"It's no big deal," Kerry said. "I've done much worse."

"I also stick to my ideals no matter what," I said quickly.

"And what are some of those ideals?" Claire asked.

"Oh, you know. Don't litter. Don't chew with your mouth open. Don't marry Charlie Sheen."

"Very good," Claire said. "For the next question, we were hoping to do something a little different."

A strange feeling gripped my stomach. Like I knew something bad was coming. "All right."

"Do you have access to a webcam?"

"Yeah."

I realized a split second too late I shouldn't have said it.

"Great!" Claire chirped. "Why don't we conduct the rest of

this interview via webcam? We had the idea yesterday, and I think it would be very helpful."

My entire body froze.

Webcam?

I could not let these people see me.

First off, I was wearing my Mexican food pajamas. The ones with little tacos, burritos, and churros all over them.

Second, I hadn't done my makeup or my hair. And I am not one of those girls who rolls out of bed and looks good. Or even okay. I'm one of those girls who rolls out of bed and looks homeless.

"Oh, no. You know what?" I said quickly. "I just remembered I left my webcam at . . . the dentist."

"At the dentist?" Taylor sounded skeptical.

"Yeah, I . . . took it in there so I could . . . post my root canal on YouTube."

"Fascinating," Kerry said in his artist-y, passionate way.

"Well, that's really too bad." Claire paused for a moment. "But I suppose we got a pretty good feel for who you are."

"I think so," I heard Taylor say.

"Definitely," Kerry put in.

"Okay then." Claire paused for a moment. "Thank you so much for taking the time to talk with us, Jesse. I will be in touch."

"Thank you so much for this opportunity," I said. "I look forward to hearing from you."

I hung up the phone and stared at it for a moment. The interview seemed to have gone fairly well, considering.

So why did I feel so weird about it?

seventeen

My office. As soon as you can get here. I have something to tell you.

Something to tell you.

I read Troy's text over and over. It seemed to get more mysterious each time.

Finally, I told Magda I was taking my lunch break, grabbed my jacket, and headed out of the coffee shop.

I arrived at Parker/Kline Creative a little after eleven-thirty.

As I walked through the huge glass doors into the lobby, the raven-haired, ruby-lipped girl at the reception desk looked up. "Can I help you?"

"I'm here to see Troy."

The girl smiled. "You must be Jesse."

I moved my head back in surprise. "Yeah."

"Troy," she said into the phone on her desk. "Jesse's here." She hung up the phone and regarded me. "He'll be right out."

"Thank you."

As I waited, I took in the scene of the office. It was so different in the daytime. The windows showed a new view. The colors seemed brighter. And there was an energy and creative pulse to the place.

"There she is."

I grinned from ear to ear at the sight of Troy. There was just something about seeing him in his domain, all cool and commanding in his striped shirt and black slacks.

"Hey, T," I said.

Troy put his arms around me, kissing me softly on the cheek in greeting. "Come on," he took my hand, "I want you to meet everyone."

As we made our way through the office, every employee seemed to want a piece of Troy.

The young guy in a blue sweater and jeans: "Hey, Troy. I got the layout for the Xlear magazine spread ready for you to look at."

The twenty-something girl in a pencil skirt and heels: "Troy, can I get your opinion on those logos today?"

The older woman in a pantsuit: "Hi, Troy. Thanks for feeding my cats while I was at the Marie Osmond doll convention."

Troy introduced me to all of them, holding my hand tightly the whole time, and I'm not going to lie, I felt all glowy and special just being next to him.

When we reached Troy's office, he handed me a Vitamin Water. As I cracked the top open, I noticed a bunch of ad materials and about a dozen bottles of nasal spray, on the table in the center of the room.

"What are you working on?" I asked.

"Xlear nasal spray," Troy said. "A potential client that's getting ready to launch a national campaign. I figure if I can dazzle them, they'll sign with us."

"Well," I pursed my lips, "you are pretty dazzling."

"You're the dazzling one." Troy moved close to me. "That's actually what I wanted to talk to you about."

"How dazzling I am?"

"That," Troy gently pushed my hair over my shoulders, onto my back, "and something else."

An intense tingle ran up my spine. "Oh?"

Troy nodded, looking excited.

So it was a good something.

Beep. Beep. Beep.

Troy pulled an apologetic face as he moved toward the phone on his desk. He checked the caller ID. "I'm so sorry. It's the Xlear people. I should get this."

"No problem." I took a seat and watched Troy in action.

"Troy Parker," he said into the phone. "Yes. Thank you for getting back to me . . ."

Man, was he hot.

As Troy talked, I picked up a notepad and started sketching. Since the nasal spray was right in front of me, I sketched a cosmopolitan-looking woman with the spray in her handbag, along with her beauty products. Then I drew a cool, suave man with the spray in the glove box of his sports cars. It was kind of fun, sketching while Troy did his thing on the phone.

I was adding some shading to the sketches when the Vitamin Water hit my bladder. I slid Troy a note.

Ladies' room?

Troy scribbled back as he continued talking, all gorgeous and multi-tasking.

Down the hall. Fifth door on the right. This might take a while. Sorry.

"No problem," I mouthed.

And it really wasn't. I liked seeing him like this.

I found the restroom easily. It was just as cool and modern as the rest of the office. Everything was automatic, the lighting was soft and flattering, and there was an area where the women kept their toiletries. And I did not go to sniff someone's tube of hand lotion and accidentally squirt it all over the mirror, if anyone asks.

As I was heading back, I passed a conference room where I heard two men arguing.

I'd just cleared the door, when a young guy with curly hair ran out and approached me. "Hey," he said, sounding desperate. "You're a woman, right?"

"Um . . ." I looked down at myself. "Yeah."

"Do you have a minute?"

I frowned. "Oh, no . . . I don't work—"

"Could you just help me out?" the guy pleaded. "I accidentally hired a focus group of men. But the product I'm researching is for women. My boss is going to kill me! It will only take five minutes."

"Okay."

"Really?"

I nodded and moved through the doorway. I could help the guy out while Troy was on the phone. "What do you need? An opinion on some soap? To hear what I think about a new nail polish color?"

My mouth snapped shut as my eyes settled on the items laid out on the table. They looked like scuba suits, but they were silver and shiny, with hoods attached to them.

"The Slim Suit Pro," the man said.

I frowned. "Uh . . ."

"I'm Kenner." The guy sat down and pointed to the gray-haired man at the other end of the table. "And that's Pete."

I waved awkwardly. "Jesse."

"Have a seat, Jesse," Kenner said.

I slowly lowered myself into a chair.

"So," Kenner crossed his legs and positioned a notepad on his knee, "the Slim Suit Pro is an outfit you wear while you're working out. It's supposed to make you sweat more. And it's weighted, making resistance moves more effective."

"All right."

"So first we need to know if you would buy a product like this?"

I stared at the suits. "Well—"

"And make sure to be completely honest."

"Okay. Well, no. I probably wouldn't buy a product like this."

Pete frowned. "Is that just because you don't work out?"

No! "It's because . . . it's kind of freaky looking."

Pete grumbled. "Who cares what it looks like? If it works, women will use it."

"I guess . . ."

Kenner tapped his pen on his pad.

"I think the only way to get an accurate assessment is to try it," Pete said, fixing his eyes on me.

Oh no. No. No. No. There was no way I was putting one of those things on.

"I think the Large will fit over your clothes," Kenner said, eyebrows raised hopefully.

"Sorry." I made an apologetic face as I stood up. "I don't think I'm the best person to do this."

Kenner looked down at his notepad. "If I lose another job, my girlfriend is outta here."

Three pathetic comments later, I was slipping into the Slim Suit Pro, looking like an alien in a really bad '70s movie.

"How do you feel?" Kenner asked.

"Ridiculous."

"That's not good."

"Of course you feel ridiculous just standing there," Pete said. "You need to do some exercises."

I was really, really starting to dislike this Pete guy.

He motioned with his hands. "Do some jumping jacks or something."

I bit my lip. "Uh . . ."

Kenner gave me a thumbs-up, his face hopeful.

And a second later, I was jumping up and down, barely getting off the ground due to the weight of the suit.

"Are you working up a sweat?" Kenner asked.

I was frying. "Yeah."

"What percentage more sweat would you say you're experiencing than you would without the suit?"

"Probably . . . fifty."

"Great." Kenner wrote on his notepad. "We can say 'Up to 95 percent more sweat.'"

I stopped jumping. "Okay. I'm taking this off now."

"Actually," Kenner said quickly. "I think we should have you do some resistance moves too."

"Good idea," Pete said. "How about a couple push ups?"

"Fine." At this point, I just wanted this little "focus group" to end.

I slowly got down on the floor. I got in push-up position. I dipped down. I pushed up. And I didn't budge. I felt like I weighed a million pounds. Kenner had to come over, roll me onto my back, and help me up.

I wiped a bead of sweat from my brow and opened my mouth to tell the guys the truth: No woman would ever buy this product.

But before I could speak, someone walked into the room.

"Good afternoon, Miss Kline," I heard Kenner say.

I hid my face and looked at Vivian through my fingers.

"How's the focus group going?" Vivian asked the guys.

Kenner flashed her a smile. "We're making headway. This *woman*," he made sure to emphasize the word, "is helping us."

"Jesse?" Vivian took another look at me.

"Hi, Vivian," I said, throwing my shoulders back like it was totally normal that I was wearing the suit.

But I'm not going to lie, I kind of felt like I should be saying, "Take me to your leader."

"What are you doing here?" Vivian asked me. "You aren't on any focus group list I've seen."

Kenner's eyes got wide with worry.

"Actually," I said, trying to cover. "Troy asked me to come in here and . . . you know . . . get focusy with it."

"Okay . . ." Vivian's eyes were slits. "So how is it going?" she asked Kenner.

"Well, the problem is . . ." Kenner looked over at me.

" . . . Jesse doesn't seem to be able to work the product."

"After all that?" I shouted, my tone saying "Et tu, Kenner?"

Vivian smiled. "Maybe it's designed for more . . . hard-core fitness buffs."

Translation: Not for a ball of lard like you, Jesse.

"Maybe I should give it a try," she said.

"Great idea boss!" Kenner said.

And just like that, she was slipping into one of the suits.

I watched, secretly looking forward to the moment she looked as ridiculous as I did.

The moment she—

Wait a minute.

She looked . . . hot.

"So this is a workout thing, huh?" she said, looking like a shiny silver surfer girl.

"It's supposed to improve your results," Kenner answered. "Not that you need more results."

With a smile, Vivian began to move around in the suit like it was nothing.

She did pushups.

She did lunges.

She did a back handspring.

Okay, fine, she didn't do a back handspring. But she may as well have.

"Well. I guess you guys don't need me anymore." I struggled with the suit for a moment, but finally slipped it off and dropped it on the table.

"Thanks, Jesse," Kenner said, eyes still on Vivian.

"No problem." I grumbled and moved toward the door.

"Hold up, Jesse." Vivian slipped out of the suit in one quick motion.

I waited by the door.

When she got to me, she walked with me out to the hall. "I'm actually kind of glad I ran into you. I was hoping we could, you know, talk. Get to know each other a bit."

"Okay. But . . ."

"It's just that Troy is a big part of my life. One of my best friends. And I'm very protective of him. I just want to make sure you're a good girl." She flashed me a smile.

"I totally understand." I think.

Vivian looked down at my feet. "Cute shoes. Very . . . casual. I wish I could be more like you, not caring about fashion, or how I look."

"Um . . ."

"So tell me more about yourself, Jesse."

I cleared my throat. "Well . . . I . . ."

"Did you go to college?"

"I did."

"Where?"

"I started out at CCP—Community College of Philadelphia. Then I transferred to Lehigh University."

"Oh." Vivian swished her hair. "Well, that's okay. Not everyone can get into an Ivy—it's *très* competitive."

"And also *très* expensive."

Vivian frowned like she didn't understand what I said. "Did you graduate?"

Translation: I bet you didn't.

"Yes," I answered.

"Well, good for you. That diploma on your wall is as good as anyone else's."

Translation: Good at getting you a job pouring coffee.

"So do you live in the city?" Vivian asked.

"Yeah. On West Elm. My brother and I have an apartment in—"

"You live with your brother? Well, that sounds . . . interesting."

Translation: Well, that sounds . . . apelike.

I nodded. "Yeah, it's—"

"There you are." Troy's voice came into my ears. "I was about to call security."

"We were just having a little *tête-à-tête*," Vivian said sweetly. "But I guess it's time to get back to work. It was very nice talking to you, Jesse."

"You too," I said.

But as Vivian disappeared from view, I couldn't help but think it was more unsettling than nice. And that I was pretty sure there was more to the whole conversation than her simply being "protective" of Troy.

"So," I fixed my eyes on Troy, "you were about to tell me something back in your office."

"Yes, I was." Troy leaned against the wall. "That campaign I was telling you about, for the nasal spray?"

I nodded.

"I'm pitching it to the company at the end of this week. In Austin."

"Austin, Texas?"

Troy nodded. "And if we get it, we'll probably stay for a week or so, to get the ball rolling."

Wait a minute. "We?"

"Vivian and I," Troy said simply.

"Oh."

"So I just wanted you to know." Troy slowly inched his hand closer to mine. "So you didn't think I disappeared on you. Because when I get back, I'm going to want to see a lot more of you."

The corners of my mouth turned up. "A lot more?"

eighteen

The second I saw the suited-up man sitting in a chair across from Darla's desk, I knew something was up.

"Hey," I said through the open office door.

Darla motioned for me to come in. "Take a seat, Jesse. Thanks for coming in early."

I gulped and plunked down beside the man in the suit.

Darla met my eye. "Gladys said she got hurt in class the other day."

"Seriously?"

"She said she thinks she tore her ACL."

I really doubted it. "Well, I wouldn't put too much stock in that."

The suit man cleared his throat.

"I asked her how it happened," Darla continued. "And she said it was when she was holding Proud Warrior pose while painting a flower on her canvas."

"I told her not to do it if it was too hard," I said.

"What's Yogainting?" Darla asked, holding one of my flyers up by a corner.

Why did that sound like a trick question? "I just thought I needed to spice up the class. You know, make it more like the ones we talked about. We've had five people join since."

"Yes, but you can't teach exercises in your class. You'd have to be certified. We'd have to increase our insurance. Your students would have to sign release forms and fill out medical forms."

An awful sinking feeling gripped my insides. Of course I'd have to be certified. Of course there was a protocol to follow. What in the world was I thinking?

"This is Mr. Hurt from Hurt & Payne, the law firm which represents the city center." Darla nodded toward him. "He has a few questions for you."

I suddenly felt like I was in really big trouble. And when I feel like I'm in trouble . . . "I stole mud from the Bliss Hotel and Spa in the Poconos!" I cried.

Mr. Hurt put a hand up to silence me. "I just need to get a few things on record."

I released a long breath, like a leaky balloon.

Mr. Hurt reached into his fancy satchel and produced a leather-bound notebook. "How many times have you integrated physical exercise into your painting class?"

"I started on the fifteenth of last month. So . . . six times."

Mr. Hurt scribbled in his notebook. "And during any of your classes, did Ms. Cohen complain of physical pain?"

"Well . . . yeah. But she always complains of physical pain."

"That's immaterial here, I'm afraid," Mr. Hurt said.

"Oh, right," I said like I actually knew what that meant.

"During any of your classes, did anyone other than Ms. Cohen complain of physical pain?"

I shook my head. "No."

"And on Thursday, March 31, did Ms. Cohen complain of pain in her leg during class?"

I thought for a minute. "No. All I remember her saying is that she had a red spot on her arm that she thought was a tick bite, and that she was 100 percent sure she had Colorado Tick Fever."

"I see." Mr. Hurt scribbled some more and then snapped his notebook shut. "That's all I need. Just make sure you stick to teaching painting, Ms. Young." He fixed me with a stare that said he would personally hunt me down if I didn't.

"Of course."

Mr. Hurt stood and headed to the door. "I'll keep you apprised of the situation. But I'm fairly certain it will resolve itself."

"Thanks," Darla said.

With a professional nod, Mr. Hurt was off.

Now, alone with Darla, I couldn't even look at her. "I'm so, so sorry," I said finally. "I was just—"

"The board voted today," she said before I could finish. "And we're going to take your class off the schedule next term."

My mouth dropped open. "Is it because of this whole—"

Darla shook her head. "They don't even know about Gladys. It just wasn't in the cards. I'm sorry, Jesse. I like you. I like your passion for art. "

I smiled weakly. "Thanks."

"At least you know you tried."

"Yeah."

Darla reached out and squeezed my hand. "I have a feeling there's something better waiting for you."

"I really hope so. And . . . I just want you to know . . . I appreciate you giving me this opportunity."

"You did a great job, Jesse." Darla smiled kindly. "But, just so you know, Mr. Hurt suggested that we cancel your classes this week. Just to let the dust settle a bit. I've already notified the students."

"Oh. Okay. I guess I'll . . . see you next week then." I slowly stood up and moved toward the door.

I felt all mixed up inside as I left the office. When the crisp evening air hit me, I decided to walk home rather than catch a cab. I just kind of felt like I could use the walk to figure things out.

And it was on that walk that something happened.

I was cutting through Colonial Square, the fastest way to get to 10th, which would connect me to Elm, when a very strange feeling came over me.

Now, here's something you should know about Colonial Square: It's a so-corny-I-can't-help-but-love-it tourist trap complete with old-timey stores and people dressed up in Colonial costumes, hocking everything from ice cream to Hello Kitty lip gloss. On the top floors of the shops are condos where no one really wants to live.

But that's the other thing you should know about Colonial Square: I did live there. Before everything happened. Back when I was planning my life with lists like Jesse and Nate's Five-Year Plan. And now that I brought him up, I guess I should also tell you, Nate still lives there. In the cozy condo we bought back . . . then.

I hadn't been back to Colonial Square in a really, really long time, with the exception of one trip to the scone shop because I was going through serious withdrawals. But the second I saw a pretty twenty-something dressed in a butter churner costume, my mind was flooded with memories.

Walking by the little pond on Sunday afternoons. Eating biscuits with fresh butter while reading the paper on the tiny condo balcony. Going down to Ye Olde Grocery Store and buying Fruit Roll-Ups for movie night.

My stroll down memory lane suddenly became painfully vivid when I saw him.

Nate.

At first, I thought my eyes were playing tricks on me. That the memories were making my mind funny.

But there he was, coming out of the candy store, a bag in his hand.

Instantly, I tried to find an escape plan.

But that's the problem with Colonial Square. It's a long, dead-end street.

Heart pounding, I quickly moved toward the closest shop. But when I pulled the handle, I realized it was locked. One look through the windows, and I saw it was completely empty.

I whipped my head to the right, and there was Nate, walking right toward me.

I searched my vicinity for any way out of this. And that's when I saw a Butter Churner Girl costume draped over the back of a wooden chair a couple feet away. The wooden butter churn was there too, resting against the chair. I had no idea why it was there, but I didn't really have time to care.

Without a second thought, I pulled on the dress, tied the apron, and hid my face beneath the bonnet. Then I sat in the chair and made like I was churning butter with the little wooden contraption.

I even added a little, "Good morrow! Fresh butter for your doublet or flummery! Fare thee well and enjoy your breeches!" for the passing tourists. (I have no idea if it made any sense. I just strung together a bunch of words I'd heard in Colonial Square over the years.)

The whole time I fake-churned, I was watching Nate in the distance. As he sat on a bench and bit into some peanut brittle. As he took his iPhone out of his pocket and began to read something. As he—

"Will you take a picture with us?" I looked to my right and saw a family in Liberty Bell T-shirts. The mom was holding out a camera.

"Um . . . sure."

I stood up and smiled for a few photos. The dad of the group tipped me five bucks.

"Thanks," I said, waving as the family walked away. "Pray remember me."

"Jesse?"

My stomach dropped to my feet.

I spun around and was suddenly facing Nate.

Nate who I hadn't seen in over a year, except for a distant

sighting at the pharmacy a few months back. Nate who I really had no idea how to be around anymore. Nate who I felt like I hadn't seen in forever, but also, somehow, felt like I'd just seen yesterday.

"Hi." I felt my whole body stiffen in discomfort.

"You got a job as a Butter Churner Girl?" Nate asked, forehead wrinkling in what looked a lot like pity.

"No," I said with an exaggerated grumble. "Actually, I'm . . . a lawyer!"

"A lawyer?" Nate scratched his head.

"Yes. With Hurt & Payne."

"Hurt & Payne," Nate said with a grin.

"It's a real firm!" I said.

"Wow." Nate nodded slowly. "How did you get through law school so quickly?"

"Oh. I . . . got on the accelerated track." I did my best lawyer-y shrug. "It's quite immaterial, actually."

"So the . . ." Nate motioned toward the costume.

"I'm here doing research for a case," I explained. "The butter churner murder."

"The what?"

"The butter churner murder." I shook my head for effect. "I'm surprised you haven't heard of it."

Nate frowned slightly. "Oh, yeah. I think I read something about that in the *Herald.*"

Huh. Maybe I could be a lawyer.

"Yeah. Well. So . . . I better—" I lowered my voice to a whisper. "—Get back to my research."

Nate met my eyes. "It was good seeing you again, Jesse."

"Yep. You, uh, too."

Nate flashed me a strange smile, and with an equally strange shrug, he was off.

I breathed a sigh of relief and watched him move away. As soon as he was out of sight, I planned to run home and throw up or something.

But when Nate reached the corner, he turned around, and started moving back toward me.

"I know you're working," he said when he reached my side. "But . . . do you have time for some tea or something?"

"I don't think so. It could really mess up discovery. And the indictment. And probably even the jury selection." Yes, I learned all those terms on *Law & Order*.

"You can't even spare a few minutes?"

"Well—" I looked at Nate. I hated how jumbled up inside the sight of him made me.

And then, in a stroke of serendipity, my phone buzzed in my pocket. I retrieved it and read a reminder to buy milk. "Sorry," I said to Nate, holding up the phone for effect. "They need me back at the office. Big legal problem. With the law."

"You still have the same phone," Nate said.

I looked down at the Motorola in my hand. "Oh, yeah."

"So I guess you have the same number."

"I really need to go, Nate." I pulled an apologetic face and turned to go.

"Would it be okay if I called you sometime?" Nate called to my back.

I spun around and faced him.

No. Absolutely not. There's nothing to talk about.

All of those words were in my head. But not one of them came out of my mouth. Instead, I just turned back around and walked away.

nineteen

At first, I didn't tell anyone about the Nate incident.

I just carried it, and the news of my art class being canceled, and everything else, with me silently. I tried to forget about it all by doing happy things like going to the farmers market with Laurel, dragging Ethan to Show Me, and raiding my favorite thrift stores on Eight-Track Tape Day.

But then I let it slip.

It was Friday afternoon, and I was at the drugstore with Laurel.

I was sniffing the Yes to Carrots lotions when I said, "This smells just like the carrot cake at my favorite place in Colonial Square. Too bad I can never, ever go there again because I might have another Nate encounter."

Laurel dropped the bubble bath she was holding. "What?"

"Bait encounter," I said quickly.

Laurel searched my face. "You ran into Nate?"

I held my head still for as long as I could. And then I nodded.

Laurel's mouth turned into an angry line. "What did Idiot Spitzer have to say? 'Sorry I ran away like a little girl.' 'Sorry I have no heart or brain.' 'Sorry I was born.'"

I fiddled with the zipper on my hoodie. "No. He just asked how I was doing and stuff."

"That loser sure has some nerve."

I didn't respond.

Laurel's face softened. "Are you okay?"

"I'm okay. It just . . . brought up a lot of stuff."

"I'm so sorry, hon." Laurel shook her head. "Do you want me to call in one of my favors with the guys from the boxing gym down the street from my apartment. Because I can."

"No."

"Okay. That's it." Laurel put an arm around me. "No more thinking about it. I'm taking you for ice cream."

"But I have dinner in less than an hour," I reminded her.

"That's right. The dinner with my mom and dad and Ethan."

I nodded. "The one you and Clint are ditching."

"Sorry," Laurel said with a shrug. "The fairy shrimp can't save themselves."

"I just really wanted you to meet Ethan."

"Trust me. You talk about him enough, I feel like I do know him."

"I do not."

"Do too." Laurel moved toward the exit. "Oh, and by the way, I almost forgot to tell you, my mom got an email from the FBI, and she said it had information on Ethan."

"What?!"

---→ ◆ ←---

"What are you reading?"

Linda snapped her head up and looked at me like she'd been caught. "Nothing."

I grabbed the paper out of her hand.

How to Profile Your Daughter's Date: Tips from the FBI
1. Pay attention to his appearance
Bad Signs: Tattoos, piercings, long hair
Good Signs: Cologne, fresh shave, respectable haircut

"What in the heck is this?" I held the paper out in front of me, eyes on Linda.

"A woman in my water aerobics class forwarded it to me. I thought tonight was a good opportunity to—"

"To profile Ethan?" My eyes were wide and incredulous.

"Why not?" Linda leaned toward me. "Does he have something to hide?"

"No! He's a perfectly nice guy."

"That's what they all say. On *48 Hours Hard Evidence*, everyone says, 'Jimbo seemed like a really great guy until he snapped one day at the IHOP and started shooting all the syrup bottles.'"

"What are you talking about?"

"I'm just saying."

Brow furrowed, I skimmed the page.

2. Observe his body language
Bad Signs: Crossed arms, slouching
Good Signs: Upright posture, handshaking
3. Check out his car
Bad Signs: Unreliable car, dirty, neglected
Good Signs: Reliable car, clean, well-maintained
4. Watch his driving
Bad Sig—

Knock. Knock. Knock.

I stopped reading abruptly and handed the paper back to Linda. "That's him. Please put that away. No profiling!"

Linda nodded and hid the sheet in a copy of *Real Simple* magazine.

Feeling a sudden smile spread across my face, I went to the door, and opened it.

"Hi." Ethan held out a houseplant, his adorable way warming me inside. "Now you have a plant."

"Yes, I do!" I took the sweet gift and hugged Ethan. "Thank you! I'm so glad you're here. And also . . . so sorry."

"Hello!" Linda seemed to pop out of nowhere.

"This is my aunt Linda," I said to Ethan.

"Nice to meet you, Linda."

Linda looked out the still-open door at Ethan's car on the curb. "Is that your car?"

Ethan nodded and shoved his hands into his pockets.

"It looks kind of old."

"Yeah."

"Do you like having an old car?"

"I . . . guess."

"Because then you can just treat it however you want? You know, toss your trash on the floor. Run over baby squirrels."

"No!" Ethan looked totally confused.

"Come on." I grabbed Ethan's arm with my free hand. "Let's go inside."

I shut the door with my foot and set the plant on the table in the entryway. I took a quick second to stare at it, basking in Ethan's thoughtfulness, and then moved toward the living room.

Linda followed behind. After a second, I noticed she was sniffling like crazy. I was wondering if she had a cold or something when I realized she was sniffing Ethan. "Are you wearing cologne?" she asked.

"I'm not really a cologne guy," Ethan said.

"Oh." Linda nodded in a way that seemed to say, "Just like most ax murders."

"Uncle Logan!" I called out. "Ethan's here."

Logan came into the living room, the newspaper crossword tucked under his arm. He regarded Ethan kindly and shook his hand. "Happy to meet you. I—"

"Wait a minute." Linda grabbed Ethan's head and pulled it down toward her face. "Is that a hole from an earring in your ear? Or just a freckle?"

"Just a freckle." Ethan shot me a startled look.

"Let's eat," I said with a clap.

A few minutes later, we were all at the dining room table, enjoying Linda's amazing spinach frittata, talking about normal, non-FBI-profiling topics.

"Jesse tells us you're a writer," Logan said.

Ethan looked over at me, sending a warm shiver up my limbs. "I'm trying."

Logan nodded. "That takes guts."

Ethan reached out and took hold of my hand. "I've actually been thinking about getting into advertising lately. It seems like one way a writer can actually make money."

I frowned. That was the first I'd heard about that.

"Well," Logan said, "money isn't everything."

"But it is something," Linda added quickly.

---→ ◆ ←---

"Thanks for being so great tonight." I plopped on the couch, enjoying the silence of the apartment.

Ethan sat down beside me and set my legs on his lap. "It was good. Your aunt and uncle are great."

"That they are." I reached out and loosely took hold of Ethan's hand. I loved how it was so familiar to me, but still new somehow. "So did you mean what you said before?"

Ethan traced the lines in the palm of my hand with his fingers. "What do you mean?"

"That thing about getting into advertising?"

"Oh. That. Well . . . maybe. I've been thinking lately that it might be time to get serious. Think about my future rather than stick with the writing thing."

"But it's your dream."

"Well, it doesn't seem to be my reality."

I shook my head. "You can't quit."

"And why is that?"

"Because I know you're going to make it."

The corners of Ethan's mouth turned up. "Okay. Not a bad reason. But . . ."

I gripped his hand almost urgently. "Promise me you won't give up."

Ethan searched my face. "How can you be so sure about me?"

"Because I know you. Because you're amazing. Because you deserve to have everything you want. And . . ." I looked down at Ethan's hand. "Because I just can."

Ethan gently pulled me toward him and kissed my forehead.

"You're my Charlie Brown," I said simply.

"I'm your what?"

I took in a breath. "When I was little, I used to watch these Charlie Brown specials on TV. And there was this one where Charlie Brown had a crush on this girl . . ."

"The little red-headed girl," Ethan said quickly.

"Right. And when the girl kissed him, Charlie Brown started flying. Like really flying. Soaring through the clouds. I totally didn't get it. So I asked my mom about it, and she said, 'That's exactly how I feel every time I kiss your dad.'"

Ethan stared into my eyes, as if transfixed by my story.

"Naturally, I thought that meant my dad had some kind of magical kissing power. So I spent the next two weeks kissing his cheeks, trying to fly. But nothing happened. I was so bummed! Eventually I actually forgot all about it. Until the first time you kissed me. And then I remembered . . . Charlie Brown."

Ethan leaned over and kissed my mouth hard, eager to help me fly.

"Promise me," I repeated softly, my lips still against his.

Ethan moved his head back. "I promise. For now."

"Good."

Ethan and I hung out on the couch for a while, watching TV, until it was almost time for him to go lock up the fitness room at his apartment building.

"I'll see you tomorrow," he said from the doorway.

"Two p.m., White Canyon Trails," I said, feeling all warm and glowy.

Ethan nodded, and with a few more kisses, he was gone.

I'd just closed the door and was about to go wash some pots that were in the sink, when I heard a knock. I smiled as I headed back to the door.

I guess he just couldn't bear to leave me for a fitness room.

But to my shock, it wasn't Ethan who was standing on the doorstep.

twenty

It was Troy.

"Hey." I blinked a few times, as if to adjust my vision. "You're back."

"I am." Troy handed me two-dozen long-stemmed roses wrapped in a gorgeous silk taffeta. They must have cost a fortune. Then he took me into a hug. "Oh. I missed you."

I couldn't hide the odd look on my face as I put the roses in a vase and set them on the kitchen counter.

"You okay?" Troy asked.

"Yeah." I shook my head. "I'm just . . . surprised."

"Well, I wanted to surprise you. Grab your coat." Troy flashed me that look of his . . . the one that always kept me on my toes.

"Where are we going?" I asked as he whisked me out of the apartment and to his BMW.

Troy raised his eyebrows conspiratorially. "You'll see."

Thirty minutes later, I was standing in his office and was suddenly reminded of the first time he'd brought me there.

"Come on," I said. "What's going on?"

"You're about to find out." Troy grabbed my hand and pulled me toward the large table in the center of the room. "Have a seat."

Brow furrowed, I sat atop the table.

With a smile, Troy moved toward a nearby easel. He removed a cloth to reveal a poster. And there they were. My sketches. The woman with the nasal spray in her handbag, and the man with the spray in his glove box, incorporated into a city scene that featured the tagline, "For Everyone with a Nose."

"No way!" My shout sounded so loud in the quiet office. "I can't believe you found those sketches!"

"Well, I'm glad I did," Troy said, a huge smile on his face. "You won this for us!"

"No."

"Yes! We're launching this fall."

"Wow." I got up and hugged Troy. "Congratulations."

"To you, too. I never would have come up with that. You're smarter than me."

I shrugged. "Well, no one's denying that."

I looked at the poster, feeling suddenly proud. My little sketches. In a national ad campaign! I shot Troy a look of glee.

"There's more," he said.

"You want David to star in the commercial?" I said with a chuckle.

"Troy?"

I looked to the door and there was Vivian, looking gorgeous in skinny jeans tucked into boots and a flowy top.

"Vivian . . . what's up?" Troy said in a clipped tone.

"Do you mind if I talk to you for a sec?"

"I'm kind of in the middle of something."

"It's urgent," Vivian said.

"Don't go anywhere." Troy shot me an apologetic look. "We have a lot more to discuss."

I nodded.

I heard the click-clack of Vivian's boots in the hall and noticed they didn't go very far. In fact, if I moved over to Troy's desk, I could probably hear the conversation.

No. That wouldn't be right.

I drummed my fingers on my legs.

And then, without another thought, I ran over to Troy's desk and put my ear against the wall.

"So have you asked her yet?" Vivian was saying.

"No." Troy cleared his throat. "I was just about to."

Ask me what?

"Do you really think this is a good idea?" Vivian asked.

"Yes, actually, I do."

"You barely know her Troy. I tried to get stuff out of her, and it was practically impossible. So tell me. What's her family like? Why is she perfectly content to work in a coffee shop? What does she have against closed-toed shoes?"

Hey!

"You came all the way down here to say this?" Troy asked.

"I came down here to tell you that you're asking for trouble," Vivian said. "And I'm going to be the one who's there for you when it doesn't work out. Just like I always am."

"This time is different," Troy said.

"This time is a phase!" Vivian practically shouted. Then she lowered her voice again. "The vegetarian John Lennon groupie who smells like peppermint and carries a bag made of hemp. Come on."

What? What!!!

"Are you done?" Troy asked.

"Will you just listen to me?!" Vivian pleaded.

"I'm going to ask her," Troy said. "And I wish that, as my friend, you could support me."

"Well, I can't."

"Come on, Viv."

"No. A friend doesn't stand by and watch another friend make a huge mistake."

Suddenly, there was complete silence.

I kept my ear to the wall, thinking maybe the two were whispering.

But then, without warning, Troy walked back into the room.

I quickly plunked myself down in his office chair and pretended to read a toothpaste ad on his desk. "Hey," I said weirdly.

"I'm sorry about that." Troy pushed his sleeves up to his elbows.

I got up from the chair and headed back to the table. "It's okay."

"So . . . as I was saying . . ." Troy looked flustered.

"You just told me, 'There's more,'" I offered. And I noticed my heart was racing a little.

Troy came to my side and then took a second to just look at me. "For a while now, I've been thinking about expanding the agency. Opening a new branch."

"Oh. Wow."

"And now that we got the Xlear campaign, we've decided that I'll oversee it from our new branch . . . in Austin."

My eyes got wide. "Texas?"

"It would only be for a few months. Once things are running smoothly . . ."

"You'll move back?"

"Austin will by my home base. But I'll be here all the time." Troy reached for my hand and grabbed it with such intensity it sent a shiver up my arm.

"When is all this going to happen?" I asked.

Troy looked into my eyes. "As soon as I say yes."

"And when will that be?"

"When you say you'll come with me." Troy paused for a second. "I know it's not on your top four places to live list. But I did find some good bike paths, farmers markets, and art galleries."

I physically moved back. I opened my mouth to speak, but nothing came out.

"Don't say anything," Troy said quickly. "Just think about it. You. Me. Austin."

"Wow. I . . ." Still. No words.

"Think about it," Troy repeated. "Take as long as you need.

As long as you say yes. And, by tomorrow night, if you can." A smile played on his lips.

I looked into his eyes, all fearless and determined.

Then, without any warning, he put a hand on my chin and lifted my lips to his, kissing me so softly I almost didn't feel it. "Run away with me," he said, his voice deep and gritty.

I narrowed my eyes, looking at him intently. "When I kiss you, I feel like I'm flying."

twenty-one

Dear Miss Young,

It is with great pleasure that I write to offer you the position of Art Teacher at Alive Academy in Austin, TX.

Attached you will find salary and benefit details as well as materials about the amazing city of Austin. Please send your written acceptance of this offer within seven days of receipt of this message, via email.

Again, it was a pleasure to interview you, and we look forward to welcoming you to our team in Austin.

Sincerely,

Claire Overton

Director, Alive Academy of the Arts

I stared at the email.

I'd probably read it a hundred times.

Austin?

I had a job offer in Austin?

How had this . . . happened?

"Hello, Jesse."

I gulped when I heard Nate's voice.

I shoved my phone into my bag. "Hi."

Nate took a seat in the chair across from me. The waitress

immediately took his order for coffee and a cinnamon apple muffin.

I held onto the strawberry soymilk smoothie in my hand for dear life. "I don't know why I'm here."

Nate got comfortable in his seat. "Because I called and asked if you wanted to have breakfast. And you said yes."

I smiled weakly.

It was true: He called last night and invited me to breakfast, I said yes, and that was why I was there.

But it wasn't the whole truth.

Deep down, I'd started to wonder if talking to Nate would help me figure out . . . things. I'd spent so long trying to heal. But what I hadn't really done was figure out how to move forward. And in a strange way, I thought looking to my past would help me find the answers I needed to move into my future.

"So how's the law game?" Nate asked.

"The what?"

"Being a lawyer?"

"How would I know?" I frowned, confused.

And then I remembered. I was a lawyer.

"Oh. Sorry." I leaned across the table and whispered. "I have to be careful. In case I'm trailed. This butter churner murder is pretty high profile."

Nate nodded doubtfully.

"What else have you been up to?" he asked after a moment.

"Well, I've been teaching an art class."

"An art class, huh? Art always was your thing."

"And how about you? How's Cheyenne?"

Cheyenne was the cute grad student Laurel spotted Nate out with three months after the divorce was final.

I did not Facebook stalk her for a little while.

"That's ancient history," Nate said. "She's working at a hospital in Pittsburg."

"Oh."

"Is there anyone in your . . ." Nate let his voice trail off.

"Actually. That's kind of one of the reasons I wanted to talk to you."

I was about to say more, when I noticed Nate checking out a pretty brunette who'd just walked into the café.

"Hey!" I said impulsively.

And then I remembered I had no reason to be insulted.

Nate returned his attention to me. "What?"

I looked down at the table. "This table is uneven! That is a legal hazard! I'm going to have to talk to the manager about this."

Nate took a sip of his coffee. "So you were saying . . ."

I stared at my hands. "I think it was good what we did. Made a clean break. Didn't think we could be friends or anything. But I also think . . . there are some things I wish I could have asked you. That I didn't get to."

Nate leaned forward slightly. "You can ask me now."

"Okay. Well. Did you ever think that . . . maybe we could have made it work? Figured out a way to deal with it all?"

Nate was quiet for a long time. "Some things aren't solvable."

I could feel tears stinging my eyes. And suddenly I wondered if this was a really, really bad idea. "But when did you decide you didn't want to try?"

I could tell Nate was getting upset by the way his mouth was twitching. "It wasn't that simple, Jess, and you know it."

"I know." Now I was upset. "I just . . . I need to know if . . . am I supposed to live my life day to day, never making plans? Or can I . . . make . . . them?"

"Don't cry. Please." Nate sounded more annoyed than concerned. "Only you know the answer to your question."

"No. Only you know! You're the one who left!"

Nate's mouth twitched even more. "Come on, Jess. Let's not go there."

I didn't know where else to go?

Did he want me to talk about the time we stumbled upon

that little restaurant with the best omelets in the world on our way home from our Honeymoon in Florida?

Or the time he put our bookshelves together backwards and tried to pretend they were supposed to look that way?

Or the time I got my foot stuck in the weird hole we had in our master bedroom closet?

"I have to go there," I said, eyes blurry. "Your life has gone on. With Cheyenne. With who knows who else. But mine has been in this halt mode. All because I don't know what the heck I'm supposed to do."

Nate looked at me across the table. Clearly he had been hoping for a different kind of talk.

"Why couldn't you handle it?" I asked suddenly.

Nate shifted in his seat. "Look, Jesse. When I ran into you the other day, I thought it was a good thing. And I wanted to talk to you. To see how you are. But I thought this . . ." He motioned like fighting. "Was over."

That was the thing. It was over for him. He left it behind when he walked away.

"Did it ever occur to you that I needed you?" I asked softly. "That I'd just found out something that turned my whole world upside down. That all I needed was someone to be willing to go through it with me?"

Nate looked into my eyes. "Did it ever occur to you that maybe I didn't want to see you suffer?"

I don't know how long we were silent after that.

But it was a pretty long time.

Finally, I grabbed my bag and was about to get up to leave.

There really wasn't anything more to say.

I'd gotten what I'd come for.

It was then that I saw Laurel burst through the café door. "There you are!" she shouted.

I sunk down into my seat, like a teenager caught in a lie.

"I knew you weren't at a classic car convention like David said! And you—" She shot Nate a look of pure venom. "What do you think you're doing, Jerk Cameron?"

"I—"

"That didn't require an answer," Laurel said, grabbing my arm. "Come on."

I got up, avoiding making eye contact with Nate.

We were just about to the door when Laurel stopped and turned around.

"She's dating someone else now, you know," she said. "Totally hot. Rich. Amazing car. And by the way . . ." She looked Nate over. " . . . That hairline has definitely seen better days."

"Miss?" A man who was apparently the café manager started walking toward Laurel. "Is there a problem here?"

"Yes, there is, sir." Laurel glared at Nate once more. "Don't you ever call her again."

twenty-two

"What are you doing?" I lifted the anti-headache ice pack from my head and stared at Laurel, who was sitting with her legs under the coffee table, typing furiously on my laptop.

"Setting up Nate's new online dating profile."

"Oh, boy. Why do I even ask?"

Laurel leaned out of the way so the computer screen was in my view.

Suddenly, I was looking at an old photo of Nate. Only it had been altered. He was holding a fluffy little dog in one hand and a copy of *Pride and Prejudice* in the other.

Beneath the photo was a dating profile.

Name: Nathaniel Banks
Favorite Hobbies: Making wishes on falling stars, walking barefoot on the beach
Favorite Movies: The Notebook, Pride and Prejudice
Favorite Books: The Twilight series, anything by Nicholas Sparks
Interested in: A woman who isn't afraid to show she really cares by sitting outside my house in her car with a pair of binoculars
Workplace: KWZL Radio, Hill Pointe, PA

Email: natebanks@kwzl.web

"Wait," I said. "That's his real email."

"I know." Laurel started typing again. "That loser obviously has too much time on his hands. I'll take care of that. Okay. I think I'm about done. 'Do you want to post your profile?' Oh, ye—"

Buzz. Buzz.

Laurel picked my phone up off the coffee table. "Hike with Ethan," she read off the screen.

I glanced at the clock. "Oh no! Is it 1:00 already?" I jumped up from the couch. "I have to get ready!"

"A hike with Ethan. This is perfect." Laurel shut the laptop and made eye contact with me. "And Jesse, listen to me. Whatever Nate said, it's complete trash. I don't want you to give any of it a second thought. Go. Hike. Have fun. And forget about everything that slime bag said."

I nodded weakly before heading down the hall.

···→ ◆ ←···

All right. This will be good. A nice hike in the fresh air.

I pulled into the dusty parking lot, parked the car, and grabbed the beat-up pack I'd brought—complete with a water bottle, dried fruit and nuts, a place to stash my wallet and keys, and some sunscreen.

When I got out of the car, I instantly spotted Ethan leaning against a wooden railing, a yellow hiking backpack on his back.

Ethan rushed up to me and threw his arms around my waist. "Hey there."

I smiled, feeling warm all over. Like when you put on a pair of pajamas you just got out of the dryer. "Hey back."

Ethan glanced at my outfit of yoga pants, purple hoodie, and tennis shoes. "You look cute," he said. "Very hiker girl."

"Oh, I just threw this together," I said with a grin.

"Ethan!"

I instantly recognized the voice as I turned my head and saw a pink-clad twelve-year-old running toward us.

Ethan looked confused. "Maddy?"

"Hi!" she said when she reached our side. "I'm glad I got here in time. My dad was driving sooo slow." She rolled her eyes. "Parentals."

"What do you mean you're glad you got here in time?" Ethan asked.

Maddy tightened her ponytail. "I saw on Facebook that you were coming here at 2:00. I thought it was totes meant to be because I'm doing an article on local outdoor activities."

"That's great, Maddy." Ethan looked over at me. "But . . . this is actually kind of a . . . date."

Maddy made a puppy dog face. "Oh. Well, my dad already left to meet me at the park at the top. So I guess I'll just hike alone. Though I've heard that's really dangerous. Hopefully my parents don't get a call tonight from someone saying I fell off the cliff." Maddy moved toward the hiking trails.

Wow. She was good.

"It's fine with me," I whispered to Ethan. "We have all day."

Ethan pulled me toward him and kissed me hard. "Just had to get my fill," he said.

Hand-in-hand, we moved to the trails and met Maddy.

"We've decided to hike up with you," I said to her.

She looked right through me and grabbed Ethan by the arm. "Thank you! You're so nice!"

Ethan grinned at me over Maddy's head, and I scanned the plastic-covered trail map in front of us. Basically, there were three trails that led up to the park. They weren't very long, but they did vary in difficulty.

"So. Which trail are we going to take?" Ethan asked.

I stared at the map. Easy: Sloth. Medium: Mole. Difficult: Jaguar.

Why did they have to name them like that? It made people who wanted the easy trail feel like losers. Why couldn't it be something more encouraging? Easy: Awesome. Medium: Awesome Plus. Difficult: Awesome Plus Plus.

"We have to hike the Jaguar!" Maddy shouted. Then she shot me a challenging look. "Unless Jesse can't handle it."

"Oh. I can handle it. I can handle it like the handlebars on my ten speed bike!"

With a weird little hop, I jogged up to the Jaguar, ignoring the smattering of warning signs posted by it, and started walking briskly up the just-wide-enough-for-one trail.

I'd show that twelve-year-old.

Ethan fell in behind me, and Maddy behind him.

"So Ethan," Maddy said without wasting any time. "Do you come hiking up here often?"

"A few times a year."

"What other kind of outdoor activities do you like?"

"I like a lot of water sports."

Suddenly, I felt Ethan grab my hand from behind me, and squeeze it, as if to send me a secret code.

Hmm. Looks like this is going to be a pretty good hike after all.

Of course, about twenty minutes later . . .

I take it back! This is the worst hike in the world!

I mean, sure, I'd never been on an actual hike before. But I had no idea my legs would be burning like they were on fire. Or that I'd be breathing like I had emphysema. Or that the inspirational, "You're almost there!" signs all the way up the trail were total lies.

What I did know was that I really needed to slow down.

So, I gradually began to lessen my pace.

"Geez," Maddy said almost instantly. "Why did you suddenly turn into a slug, Jesse? Is this hike too hard for you? Should we have done the Sloth?"

"No. I'm fine."

As if to prove the point, I sped up a little bit.

Within a few minutes, I started seeing little red and black spots.

"So, does anyone need a break?" I asked, making sure my tone said, "Because I don't, but I'd be willing to stop if someone else needs to."

"Why would we need a break?" Maddy said. "We barely started. When my PE class hiked this trail, this kid Justin had a broken leg, and he went all the way up without stopping."

"Okay," I said breezily. "I was just checking."

"So—" Maddy said to Ethan.

And that's when I hatched a plan.

"Snake!" I shouted suddenly.

"Ahh!" Maddy screamed.

"Where?" Ethan said, looking at his feet.

"Right over there." I moved my hand in the air willy-nilly. "A yellow speckled mountain snake."

"I hate snakes," Maddy said, her voice squeaky.

"It's okay," I said calmly. "They're not poisonous. But they do bite. Luckily, they're fast movers, and they'll pass you in no time. So if you spot them you just have to stop. And stand perfectly still. For three to five minutes."

Maddy froze in place.

"Where did you hear this?" Ethan asked.

"Oh . . . on . . . *The View.* They know about things before everyone else."

Ethan brushed his fingers against mine, making me momentarily forget about my legs, my lungs, and everything else. "I guess we should stay still then."

I smiled and enjoyed the glorious break.

"Do you think he's gone?" Maddy whispered after a few minutes of silence.

"Probably," I said, kicking myself for saying "three to five minutes."

Maddy retrieved a water bottle from her pack and took a swig. "Hey, I think I can see the park."

Ethan stretched his neck. "Oh yeah. There it is."

Of course. After all that, we were a few steps from the park.

We all took nice long sips of water as we headed for the park, where a few other hikers, and other people who had driven up, were enjoying the spectacular view.

"There's my dad," Maddy said. "I guess I better go."

I gave a little wave. "See you later, Maddy."

"I hope not." She turned to Ethan. "Thanks for all your help, Ethan."

"You're welcome, Maddy."

The second he said her name, Maddy's cheeks turned pink. "Bye," she said before jogging off.

When we were finally alone, Ethan pulled me toward him and kissed my lips. I could feel the warmth of his body, the swift beat of his heart, and it did all kinds of crazy things to my insides. "Well," he said. "Here we are."

"Here we are," I repeated.

Ethan took my hand and led me to a smooth rock that was off a bit from the rest of the park. He took off his pack and removed a blanket that he spread out for us to sit on.

I sat beside him and looked out at the breathtaking view. I could see for miles. "It's so amazing up here."

"My family used to hike up here a lot when I was growing up."

I sipped my water and resisted the urge to pour it on my face. "That's a tough hike for a kid."

And for an adult.

And for a yak.

Ethan grinned. "I was a tough kid."

"Aw. You must have been such a cute little boy."

"When I was in seventh grade," Ethan said in that way of his that let me know I was in for a great story, "I brought home a progress report that said I was failing science. My mom went *ballistic*. Then, the next afternoon, my dad and I came up here. He said they were so upset because they knew I was smart enough to be anything I wanted to be. He was so sure about me."

I sat cross-legged on the blanket. "Were you not so sure about you?"

Ethan shrugged. "Have you ever been totally sure of yourself?"

"I think I was when I was younger. But now . . ." I stared into the distance. "I don't think you can be totally certain about anything."

Ethan looked over at me. "I don't know if I agree with that."

"What are you totally sure about?"

"It used to be that I was going to be a writer. Lately, though, I haven't been so certain about that." He paused. "But then I met this girl in a café. Beautiful. Funny. Blonde." Ethan grinned playfully.

I twisted up my lips. "Hey."

Ethan grinned his adorable, boyish grin. "I was certain I wanted to talk to her. Wanted to know her. And as I began to know her, I was certain I had never known anyone like her. That everything with her was better than anything without her. That I was better with her."

I blinked, moved by Ethan's words.

"I'm in love with you, Jesse," he said, the words so beautiful, so right.

I held his gaze, feeling the whole world fall away. "I love you too."

"And I'm also sure about something else." Ethan reached into his pocket and removed a small velvet box.

My heart pounded in my chest.

Ethan got down on one knee. "I'm sure I want to spend the rest of my life with you." He paused for a moment. "Marry me?"

Ethan opened the ring box in a way so sweet, so romantic, so . . . Ethan, I felt like my heart would explode. I stared at the simple, beautiful ring in the box and everything in me wanted to say one thing.

And yet . . .

"Ethan." His name was almost painful to say. "You are so . . . amazing."

Ethan's smile fell instantly. The excitement was gone, replaced with a look of fear.

I hated myself for putting that look on his face. For letting things get this far with someone like him. Someone who wanted the long, happy life with four kids, a dog, and a house in the burbs. Someone who had all those dreams, those plans. The ones I'd had to give up.

"Amazing . . . enough to marry?" Ethan asked, his smile pained.

I reached out and took hold of his hands, tears pooling in my eyes. "I don't . . ." Everything was blurry. "I don't think . . ."

"I know it's fast." Ethan got off his knee and sat so he was facing me. "But I know it's right."

I blinked wordlessly.

Ethan looked away. "But . . . if it isn't right for you . . ."

"That's not . . . there's just . . . so much we don't know about each other."

"So tell me. All of it. Nothing is going to change the way I feel about you."

I opened my mouth. To tell him everything I'd been too afraid to tell him. But the words got caught in my throat. I just couldn't bear to see the change in his eyes once he knew.

"Tell me this," Ethan said, breaking the silence. "Do you love me? I mean, really, honestly love me."

Tears fell onto my cheeks. "Yes."

Ethan pulled me toward him. "Then talk to me."

The tears intensified. So much that my body started to shake. "I . . ."

"Come on, Jesse. What is it you aren't telling me? I know there's something. Just give me the chance to know what's going on with you."

"Ethan." I leaned back, putting distance between us. "I can't . . ."

"Can't?" he asked. "Or won't?"

"Can't," I choked out. "I just can't be who you need me to be."

I jumped to my feet, and suddenly I was running, fast, through the park and down the trail.

It turned out, it was a lot easier to get down than it was to get up.

The whole way, the words I couldn't bear to speak, pounded in my brain. My secret. The one I didn't think we could survive.

What I never could have known, though, was that Ethan had a secret of his own.

One that would change everything.

twenty-three

Mazzy Star, on repeat.

No light except for a flickering candle.

A pile of wadded-up Kleenex on the duvet.

And a mascara-stained pillow.

That ought to give you a little insight into my state.

I'd been in my room for hours, and I was a complete mess. Because I'd made a mess.

I'd tried to keep my distance and tell myself I was "playing the field." But with Ethan there was no playing. It was real. From the moment I met him.

Problem was, he was the wrong kind of guy. A bright-eyed planner and dreamer. And I needed to stay away from planners and dreamers.

"Jesse?"

I wiped my nose on my sleeve and sniffled. "Yeah?"

David cracked the door and poked his head inside. "I made you some soup."

I sat up on the bed and waved him in.

"So do you want to talk about it?" David asked as he set the bowl of rice noodle soup on my nightstand.

"I just . . . not yet."

"Okay. Well, I'll be out in the living room watching *White Christmas* if you need me."

It was a valiant effort on David's part.

Usually, nothing perked me up faster than a musical.

When I was twelve years old and Russell Gavin broke up with me because I "wore too many jelly bracelets," I rushed home from school and watched *The Sound of Music*.

When I was sixteen, and my date to the Spring Fling ditched me because I wouldn't dance to "Da Dip" with him, I took a cab home and consoled myself with a viewing of *My Fair Lady*.

When I was seventeen and got a 740 on the English portion of the SAT and a 440 on the math, I watched *West Side Story* over and over.

But this? This was too big even for a musical.

David touched my hand in a brotherly way. "And I went out and bought a box of Creamsicles."

I faked a smile. "Maybe after I eat the soup."

"All right." David got up and headed for the door.

A minute later, I heard the sound of the opening credits of *White Christmas*. I sunk back into my pillows, put on some headphones, and listened to Radiohead's "Fake Plastic Trees," Slow Reader's "Anesthetic for the Amputee," and a bunch of Elliott Smith.

The whole time, I went over everything in my mind.

All that had unfolded in the past twenty-four hours.

After a while, it was clear.

There really was only one thing I could do.

So, tears burning my eyes, I dug in my desk for a piece of paper and a pen and wrote the hardest letter I ever had to write in my life.

Dear Ethan,

I know I probably should tell you what I'm about to tell you face-to-face. But that's the problem. I know if I see you, I won't be able to do it. So, I have to do it this way.

Ethan, I love you. But I can't marry you. Please, please trust me when I tell you this is the right thing. It's the only thing. I know I let things go too far, and for that, I am so truly sorry.

Seeing you again will only make this harder, so please just accept my answer. I know you're going to have the beautiful life you dream of. I'll always be grateful to you for everything you are and everything you've been to me.

Jesse

Without allowing time to talk myself out of it, I put the letter in an envelope, slipped on a hooded jacket, and snuck outside while David was in the bathroom. Then I ran to the car and drove to Ethan's apartment, parking half a block away so I wouldn't be seen.

I stood on his doorstep for a long time, my hands shaking.

But finally I set the envelope on the welcome mat, rang the bell, and hid in a concealed corner of the hall until I heard the door open and close.

I waited a few more minutes and exited through the back of the building, leaving a trail of tears on the hallway floor.

Back in the car, I got out my phone and typed an email.

Dear Miss Overton,

Thank you very much for your offer.

I am writing to officially accept the position of Art Teacher at Alive Academy of the Arts in Austin, Texas.

I can start in two weeks.

Sincerely,

Jesse Young

twenty-four

Troy. Okay. Let's run away. Jesse.

twenty-five

~~Bon Voyage!~~ *You're Dead To Me*

"Laurel." Aunt Linda stared at the handwritten change to the banner on the wall and frowned. "What did you do?"

"What needed to be done." Laurel said, shooting me a hateful look.

She'd been furious with me ever since I told her about my new job in Austin.

My new job in Austin.

That's so crazy to say.

Even crazier was the whirlwind week I'd had. Putting my written notice on Magda's desk, and pretending I hadn't heard her shout in celebration when she found it. Packing up my stuff, along with a few things of David's I hoped he wouldn't notice were gone. Online apartment hunting, which is kind of scary if you read the stuff people post on apartment rating websites. (A couple examples: I hope you like roaches. I think my neighbor is a drug dealer.)

And now, there I was, at the surprise Bon Voyage party Linda and Logan had put together. I'd had absolutely no idea they were doing it and was so moved when I saw everyone I loved in their living room. The family. Magda. My entire art class.

"Come on, Laurel," I said. "You've got to talk to me eventually."

Laurel pressed her lips together determinedly and walked away.

"She'll come around." Uncle Logan put an arm around me. "We just got so spoiled living near you all this time."

I made a desperate face. "We'll video chat every weekend! And I'll be back all the time. That was part of the deal!"

"Lies!" Laurel shouted over her shoulder. "You'll go to Austin and disappear."

Eldon, who was nearby checking the TV for evidence of surveillance equipment, rushed up to Laurel. "You know about the recent alien abductions down there too?"

Laurel frowned and walked toward the trays of hors d'oeuvres on the dining room table.

I sidled up to Bill and Terry, who were standing in front of the fireplace. "Hey, guys. Thanks so much for coming."

"We wouldn't have missed it," Bill said. "When your aunt called, I immediately put the date and time in my BlackBerry so I wouldn't forget."

Terry glared at her husband. "So you do know how to use your BlackBerry calendar, then? Why did I get a card fourteen days after my birthday that said, 'Sorry I forgot your b-day. Here's fifty bucks.'"

I shifted on my feet. "Um . . . well . . . I better . . ."

"Jesse!"

I turned around and silently thanked Gladys for her impeccable timing.

"Gladys! How are you?"

"Awful," she moaned. "I'm so tired. And I've been having these weird hot flashes. And mood swings like you wouldn't believe."

"Oh. So you think you're going through . . ." I smiled awkwardly—"You know."

Gladys nodded. "I looked it up online. It's either bipolar disorder or malaria."

"I'm gonna miss you, Gladys!" I put an arm around her and squeezed her shoulder.

"Ouch! That's my bad shoulder!" She touched it and then the other one. "No, wait. No it's not."

"Okay everyone!" Aunt Linda said from the front of the room. "Can I have your attention? It's time for some gifts!"

"Aw." I felt a swell inside. "You guys didn't have to . . ."

Jerome quickly moved toward a large gift hidden behind the piano. "Here, Jesse. From your art class."

Smiling widely, he handed me a large, flat package wrapped in shiny blue paper.

"Wow." I ripped into the paper. "This is so sweet."

Everyone watched intently as I revealed the present, which was a frame that featured six drawings of me, all done by my art students.

They were . . . interesting.

In the one by Jerome, my head was shaped like a peanut, and my arms and legs were exactly the same length.

In the one by Bill, I was a tiny stick figure, waving from the front seat of the Corvette he'd drawn for the class we had weeks ago.

And in the one by Eldon, the drawing of me was actually pretty good, but there was a UFO hovering over my head.

"Wow . . . These are . . ."

"We just wanted to let you know how much we appreciate what you taught us," Jana said.

And that's all it took. I immediately felt myself well up. "Thank you."

"I have something too." Magda kissed me on the cheek as she handed me a box.

Inside I found a framed copy of the Employee of the

Month poster Magda had made. Except she'd made a couple changes.

Sugar House Coffee Best Employee Ever
Name: Jesse
Age: 31
Favorite Movies: Yellow Submarine, White Christmas
Favorite Bands: Sufjan Stevens, Death Cab for Cutie
Favorite Foods: Creamsicles, Gardenburgers
Sign: Libra
Status: Going to be Missed by Everyone

Magda and all of my co-workers, even the busboy I almost froze to death, had signed the poster.

I hugged Magda. "Thank you so much. For everything."

"We have something too," Linda said. "From the whole family."

Laurel grumbled. "Not from me."

Linda shook her head and handed me an envelope with a $500 Home Depot gift card inside.

"For curtain rods or whatever you need in your new place," Logan said.

Tears pooled in my eyes. "I . . . you're . . ." I struggled to find the right words to adequately express what everyone's kindness meant to me. And how much I was going to miss them all.

And just then, Laurel shoved a box in front of my face. "This is from me."

I couldn't help but smile.

I knew she'd come around.

I knew she couldn't stay mad forever.

I ripped into the gift and found a white T-shirt inside, wrapped in the tissue paper from Memor-Tees, the little kiosk in the mall where you can make your own T-shirts with photos and sayings on them.

My heart warmed as I thought about what might be on it.

Maybe that photo of us when we were little kids, jumping hand in hand off the side of the community pool, and some really moving quote about how cousins are friends who share your DNA.

Or . . .

My guessing stopped the second I unfolded the tee and held it up in front of me.

Top 3 Worst Traitors in History:
Benedict Arnold
LeBron James
Jesse Young!!!

"Laurel," Linda said in a scolding voice.

"What?" Laurel crunched on a celery stick.

I set the T-shirt back in the box gingerly and looked out at the crowd. "I love it all! Thank you so much everyone!"

The guests looked at me and Laurel for an awkward second, and then Bill started a spontaneous round of "For She's a Jolly Good Fellow." Everyone joined in, including Laurel. Granted, she made up her own words.

After another half hour or so, the party started to wind down, and I found myself on the couch, talking to Linda. "I still can't believe you did all this. It means so much to me."

And there were those darn tears again.

"Well, you mean so much to us."

"I just wish Laurel wasn't so mad at me." I sighed and looked down at the traitor T-shirt, which I'd slipped on over my henley. "I mean, she's the one who told me about the art job!" I shouted the last part so Laurel could hear me.

"Yeah," she shouted back. And then she locked eyes with me. "But you're not going because of a job or a guy or even an adventure. You're going because you're running away."

---> ◆ ◆---

I was in my pajamas, exhausted and packing a few stray kitchen items, when my cell rang in the living room.

I let it go to voice mail and went to check it when I was done.

The second I saw the name on the screen, my heart ached. Ethan.

He'd called a few times since I left the letter on his doorstep, but he'd never left a message.

Until now.

I put the phone to speaker and listened, pulse quickening.

"Jesse. I really don't know what to do. I thought I'd give you a little time. But now I'm confused and hurt and don't understand . . . what happened. So I just think I'm going to keep calling and leaving messages. I don't know. I just . . . I miss you. I'm still here. And I miss you."

When I looked up, David was standing in front of me.

"Don't," I said quickly.

David put his hands in his pockets. "I didn't say anything."

I dropped a stack of cookbooks into a box on the coffee table. "It's what you're thinking."

"What am I thinking?"

I released a breath. "That I made the wrong decision."

"Are you sure that's not what you're thinking?" David asked.

"I just . . . can't be here." I looked around. "Everything reminds me of . . . everything. After I'm gone, it'll all be easier."

"For him or for you?"

"Come on. Not you too." I sighed pitifully and sat down on the couch. David walked over and sat next to me.

"You want to know what I'm really thinking?" His eyes were full of brotherly love and concern.

"Do I have a choice?"

"I think you're an amazing person. And I think you deserve to be happy."

I stared down at my hands.

"And I think if you don't tell Ethan the truth, about everything, you'll never be as happy as you could be. No matter what happens."

twenty-six

Someone was sending me weird texts.

Don't do it.

You're making a mistake.

Back out before it's too late.

I scrolled through and deleted them as I pretended to listen to Kenner talk about how great the University of Texas football team is.

We were in a conference room at Parker/Kline, where the whole agency was celebrating the opening of the new branch. There was soft music, canapés, and champagne flutes filled with a new energy drink called Dynamite, which the agency was representing. Somehow Troy had disappeared into the crowd, and I was left talking to Kenner.

Clink, clink, clink.

Everyone turned to the woman I recognized as the one who thanked Troy for watching her cats. "I would like to make a toast! When I first joined Parker/Kline four years ago, we were in a tiny little office space on 32nd Street. Our biggest client was Chucky's Chicken Shack."

Everyone in the room laughed.

"And now just look at us." The woman was getting teary. "Troy's off to Austin to open a new branch. And . . . and . . . I just have to say, it's an honor to be part of Parker/Kline."

"Hear, hear," everyone shouted jovially.

The sound of clinking glasses filled the room.

"Where is Troy?" Kenner asked, brow furrowed as he looked around.

"That's a good question." I set my glass down. "I'd better go find him."

After a fruitless scan of the conference room, I searched the hall outside. It was then that I heard his voice.

"Can we not do this right now?" he was saying.

I inched toward the sound and concealed myself behind an open door.

"You're leaving tonight," a voice that was distinctly Vivian's said. "And she's leaving tomorrow. We have to do this now."

Troy let out a long sigh. "We've been over all of this already, Vivian. I know what I'm doing."

"No, you don't." Vivian was silent for a moment. "It's either her or me."

My jaw dropped to the floor.

"You've lost it," Troy said.

"No, Troy. You've lost it. And so I'm telling you, if you stay with Jesse, I'm out."

"What do you mean out?"

"I'm out of this company. And out of your life. I'm not going to stand by and watch this girl ruin your life."

"This girl is the best thing that ever happened to me!"

"No," Vivian said succinctly. "You're completely deluded. And I just want you to know, if she gets on that plane tomorrow, I'm gone."

"Come on, Vivian."

"No. That's it. You know what you're doing is wrong. Deep down I know you do. And so this is how it's going to be."

"You're crazy." I heard Troy move toward the door. "I'm going back to the party."

"Fine." Vivian's footsteps seemed to follow Troy's. "But I'm dead serious Troy."

Realizing they were a lot closer than I thought, I quickly began to run away. But I didn't go quite fast enough. They spotted me moving down the hall.

"Jesse?" Troy called after me, his voice tight.

I spun around and pretended to be shocked to see him. "Oh my gosh! Troy!"

"Hi, Jesse," Vivian said, flashing me a fake smile.

I may or may not have wondered if I could knock those pearly white teeth of hers out.

"So," Troy said worriedly, "what are you doing out here?"

"I was looking for you."

"Well, here he is," Vivian said, still smiling. "And just in case I don't get to see you again, let me just say, I hope you have a good flight."

Translation: I hope your plane's engine dies and you plummet to your death.

"Thanks, Vivian." I could feel my hands form fists at my sides.

"Just as long as you don't get to the airport and decide to change your mind!" Vivian said with a fake laugh.

I opened my mouth to say, "Oh, that won't happen, you psychopath."

But, for some reason, nothing came out.

⟶ ◆ ⟵

Oh no.

This is a problem.

I just saw Ethan.

For the third time since I got to the airport.

Time #1: The Ethan at the Skycap who turned out to be a fifteen-year-old kid with a mohawk.

Time #2: The Ethan buying a bag of Skittles who was actually an elderly woman.

Time #3: The Ethan inside Starbucks who, as it so happened, was a cardboard cutout of one of the Jonas Brothers. I have no idea which one.

By the time I got to the Delta Airlines check-in area, I was on high Ethan alert and kind of freaking out.

I take that back. I was totally freaking out.

I slapped my cheeks, as if to bring me to reality.

I was moving.

To. Day.

I had quit my job and accepted a new one. I had put a deposit down on an apartment. All of my possessions were currently on a truck on the way to that apartment.

I took a few deep breaths and checked in at the self-serve kiosk and then waited in line to check my bag.

When I got to the front, the agent, a woman named Abby, greeted me. "Where to today?"

"Austin." I held out my driver's license. But then I snapped it back. "I think."

I stared at the license in my hand, feeling suddenly light-headed.

Abby blinked. "You're not sure where you're going?"

"No. I'm sure about where my ticket says I'm going. But I'm not sure I want to . . . do this."

"Not sure you want to check baggage?"

"No. It's just . . ." I leaned on the counter for support. "I'm just starting to feel like this is all wrong."

Abby frowned.

I lowered my voice. "What if someone offered you something really appealing and you said yes. But then as you actually started to do that thing, you couldn't help but feel really weird about it. Like maybe it was all wrong."

"I . . . don't know." Abby looked at my red suitcase. "How many bags are you checking today?"

I released a breath. "But see, that's the thing. Do I feel wrong about it because it's wrong? Or do I feel wrong about it because it's against my nature? You know, because I usually like to take my time with things?"

Abby looked at the long line behind me. "I'm . . . not sure. But if you're not checking any bags today, I'm going to have to ask you to let me help the next person in line."

"I should just go for it, right? Go with the flow. I wanted to be more impulsive. This definitely fits the bill."

"Definitely," Abby said with a nod.

"You're right." I slapped my license down on the desk and put my bag on the scale.

"Just one bag?" Abby asked as she typed on her computer.

"Just one."

Abby attached a tag to my suitcase, and set it among a cluster of bags waiting to go on the conveyor belt. After a few more clicks on the computer, she handed me my baggage claim ticket. "Okay. You're all set. Gate D-5. Have a good flight. And good luck with . . . everything."

I slung my carry-on tote over my shoulder and walked away. As I headed for the security checkpoint, I realized I needed my license again. I dug for it, and suddenly came upon a large manila envelope.

What in the world?

I removed the envelope and saw a sticky note from David attached.

Jesse,

Ethan's sister dropped this off for you a few days ago.
Call me when you land,
David

Brows knit together, I ripped the envelope open. Inside I found a few sheets of paper. The first was a note from Sarah.

Hi Jesse,

   My kids have been asking me to give these to you since you came over. So I was in the neighborhood today and thought I'd drop them off. We really had a wonderful time meeting you!
Sarah

The next page in the envelope was a drawing. A stick figure, crayon-colored, picture of me—with wavy hair, two pink cheeks, and big brown eyes. Underneath it was a message scribbled in adorable little girl handwriting.

Dear Jesse,

   I had fun playing with you. When are you coming over again?
Love,

Hayley Elizabeth Walters

I felt a prickling in my heart as I flipped to the next picture, this one by Conner. It was all black and blue lines, with triangle people wielding guns and masks. He too had scribbled a message.

   Jesse. You should play Ninja Tag with Uncle Ethan and me next time. It's fun.

I traced the edges of the sweet drawings with my finger and thought back to that day. The day I saw, in full living color, that Ethan was undoubtedly the kind, amazing, wonderful man I thought he was. The day I began to realize that he was so good . . . I was bad . . . for him.

Tears filled my eyes as I thought back to that moment in the car, when he gave me Firefly, and I couldn't bear to tell him the truth.

Suddenly, my whole body seemed to get hot.

And I realized something with such clarity it was like someone actually said it to me: All this time I really, truly had myself convinced I was doing what was best for him. But the truth was, I was doing what was easiest for me.

Just like David said.

Suddenly, I shoved the papers into my bag, and ran like the wind in the complete opposite direction of the departure gates.

Heart racing, I stopped in front of the Arrivals/Departures board and frantically tried to call Ethan.

No answer.

I was just about to try again, when I heard a deep male voice behind me. "Excuse me?"

My heart leapt.

And as I slowly turned around, I knew I would always, always remember this moment.

"Yes," I said, my eyes meeting Ethan's.

Wait. That's not Ethan. It's some guy with a ponytail.

"You're standing on my jacket." The guy pointed to a denim jacket on the floor, an irritated look on his face.

"Oh no." I moved my feet. "I'm so sorry."

And with that I dropped my phone in my bag and dashed toward the automatic doors.

So maybe I wouldn't always remember that moment.

But the ones coming up?

Oh yeah.

twenty-seven

Ethan wasn't home.

So I broke in.

Which was a lot harder than it looks on TV.

Trust me.

Finally, after what seemed like forever, there he was.

"I thought you left," he said from the doorway.

I shifted on the couch cushions. "I thought I would."

Ethan shut the door behind him and tossed his keys on the bookshelf.

I took in and released a breath. "I have to tell you something."

As the words came out, I realized that for the first time, I felt no fear. Nerves, yes. Anxiety, maybe a little. But fear? No.

"I have to tell *you* something." Ethan walked to his desk, where he picked up a stack of papers.

I watched him as he moved. Man, I missed him so much. "Is that your movie?" I asked as he approached me.

"Yes. And." Ethan sat down beside me and held out a crisp white letter. On the top was the letterhead for Barbara Vanderbilt Agency.

As soon as I saw the word *Congratulations*, my mouth dropped open. "Oh, Ethan. You did it!"

"*We* did it," Ethan said with conviction.

I frowned and tilted my head to the side.

Ethan handed me the script. I set it on my knees and looked down at the title: *Girl Meets Troy*.

"What's it about?" I asked.

"My girlfriend's boyfriend," Ethan said.

"Your . . . huh?"

Ethan looked at me, and I saw a fire in his eyes I'd never seen before. "The day I met you, something . . . happened in me. You changed me. This script I've been writing—this is us. My agent says it has passion. And heart." He paused for a moment. "It's the best thing I've ever written."

I looked down and began to read.

The movie was about a girl named Jesse and a guy named Troy.

Time seemed to stand still as I soaked up the story.

I read about Troy coming into a coffee shop and meeting Jesse.

I read about their first date at a fancy French restaurant called Rue 8.

I read about their second date, golfing and eating at the golf club restaurant.

I read about a girl named Vivian, Troy's business partner, who so obviously had feelings for him, but cloaked it in being "a good friend." (I saw right through it.)

I read about Troy taking Jesse to the mountains.

And I read about him asking her to run away to Austin with him.

As I read, I suddenly remembered the night Ethan told me he was working on something new. This was it.

I put my finger on the page to hold my spot and looked up at Ethan. "This guy, Troy. He's . . . not really like you."

Ethan shrugged in his adorable self-deprecating way. "Yeah. I had to change that. No one wants to watch a movie about a guy like me."

I couldn't help but laugh. "And this Vivian girl? How did you write someone so . . . awful?"

"I had a few experiences to draw from, thanks to Maddy." Ethan smiled. "But as far as the character, I just thought of what you'd do or say and wrote the complete opposite."

Oh, wow. If I wasn't already madly in love with the guy, that just might have done it.

"Wow, Ethan. This story . . . it's amazing."

"I changed the ending, though." Ethan's face took on a hopeful expression. "Instead of leaving that letter on my door-step, you show up, say yes, and we run away together." He shrugged one shoulder. "Everyone loves a happy ending."

I blinked, my eyes on the pages in my lap.

This was my chance.

"What if I'm not a happy-ending kind of girl?" I asked as I looked up.

Ethan furrowed his brow.

"I love you, Ethan. With everything in me. And I know you could tell there was something I wasn't telling you. I know you could feel me pulling away. And I am so sorry."

"It's okay." Ethan looked at me with such love, such concern I felt tears burn my eyes.

"It wasn't that I didn't trust you," I continued. "It was that I hate that it's part of me. I hate that it happened. I hate that it changed everything."

"What changed everything?" Ethan searched my face as if to look for clues.

I braced myself. "About a year after I got married, I was at work one day when I felt like I was going to pass out. And then I got this awful pain in my stomach, the worst pain I'd ever felt. Someone called an ambulance, and I woke up in a hospital recovery room."

Ethan reached out and grabbed my hand.

"The first thing I remember seeing is Nate's face. And I swear he was looking at me differently. I looked down at myself almost thinking I'd lost a limb or something. But that wasn't what I lost."

Ethan was completely motionless.

"I lost the life I planned. The ten little fingers and ten little toes. The birthday parties. The building snowmen in the back-yard. I'll never have any of that. And Nate decided he wasn't willing to give it all up. And the thing is, I couldn't really blame him."

Ethan fixed his eyes on mine, shaking his head. "Why didn't you tell me?"

"Because I was scared. Because I didn't want you to look at me differently too. "

"I'm not him, Jesse."

I looked down. "I know."

Ethan squeezed my hand like he never wanted to let go. "All I want is you. I don't need anything else."

I smiled feebly. "Maybe not now. Maybe not in a few years. But you deserve to be with someone who can give you the life you've dreamed of." I moved my hands out of Ethan's. "So. I couldn't leave without telling you that."

"Where are you going?" Ethan asked, his voice breaking slightly.

"I took a job in Austin." I laughed a pained laugh and looked down at the script. "Kind of ironic."

Ethan tapped the pages urgently. "Jesse. I never could have written this without you. Because I've never been as happy as I am when I'm with you. You say I deserve to be with someone who can give me the life I dreamed of. Well, you're better than any dream I could've come up with."

"Ethan, I've seen you with Conner and Hayley. I've heard you talk about your future family." A tear fell on my cheek. "I'll never be a mother."

"Of course you will." Ethan looked at me with such pure simplicity I felt my breath catch. "We'll adopt. We'll steal Hayley and Conner and drive to Canada. We'll get dogs or cats or goats. We'll get a pool or a cotton candy machine and lure all the neighborhood kids over."

More tears fell.

But now, they were a different kind of tears.

In all my wildest hopes, my craziest dreams, those were exactly the words I hoped a man would say to me. Because deep down I believed I would find a way to be a mother. The way that was meant for me.

But I never, ever thought I'd find someone who believed that too.

Now I had.

I could be a dreamer, a planner. I could be with a man who was a dreamer and a planner. And when our dreams and plans didn't turn out exactly the way we hoped, he'd complain with me, maybe even cry with me, and then he'd help me find new dreams and new plans.

Because he was the right man.

"I love you so much." I threw my arms around Ethan and breathed him in. I wasn't sure I would ever be able to let go.

"I love you." Ethan kissed my forehead and every inch of me felt it. "Do you remember our first date?"

I sunk into him. "Of course."

Ethan kissed me again and stood up. He walked toward a bookshelf near the kitchen. "We were in the baseball field and you told me life doesn't turn out the way we expect."

"Yeah."

"Well, you were right. I didn't expect to find you." Ethan grabbed something off the shelf and came back to my side. "You say you're not a happily-ever-after kind of girl. But I think . . . if you say yes, we can have our happily ever after." With a glint in his eye, Ethan held out a ring I immediately recognized.

"Happily ever after?" I asked, my voice full of emotion. "Really?"

Ethan nodded. "Trust me. I'm a screen writer."

I stared at the ring, at Ethan's fingers holding it out for me, and took in the beautiful moment. "Yes," I said, tears in my eyes.

Ethan put the ring on my finger and kissed me so good I almost couldn't breathe.

And suddenly, I was flying.

Cheeks flushed, I kissed him a few more times then rested my head on his shoulder, looking down at the ring. "I'm sorry, but . . . Troy? Couldn't you come up with a better name than that?"

Ethan shook his head. "Everybody's a critic."

I grinned and laced my fingers through his. "Why didn't you change anything about me?"

"I couldn't change you." Ethan tucked a strand of hair behind my ear. "You're perfect."

And it was right then, in that moment, that I decided that when I told you this story, I'd have to include Ethan's story.

Because for the first time in my life, someone didn't want to change a single thing about me. Because in Ethan's creation of the "perfect" guy and "perfect" dates, he left me exactly as I was.

And I wanted you to see that.

I wanted you to read his movie—well, the book adaptation of his movie, which is going to be released a few months after the movie—and see that he knew me. He saw me. He loved me.

And, yes, I do realize that in the process I might have made you a little frustrated with me. And I'm really sorry about that. I mean, you've been reading this whole time thinking I was dating two guys at once. But I swear, I've never dated two guys at once.

Well, except for on Valentine's Day in third grade. But that was only because Nick gave me chocolates and Tom gave me a heart necklace.

Ethan set the script on the end table. "My agent wants me to write a sequel."

"Really?" I asked, eyes wide. "What's that one going to be about?"

"Actually . . ." Ethan took my face into his hands and kissed me. "I was hoping you could help me with that."

after

Dear Jesse,

*I was surprised to see your wedding announcement in
The Herald. I've been thinking a lot these past few months.
About the last time I saw you. I know I told you I left because
I didn't want to see you suffer. But I think we both know I
left because I wanted life to turn out my way. But that's the
thing, Jesse. I gave up something I had, something I loved,
for something I may never have. And I realize now what a
mistake that was. You asked me if I ever thought we could
make it work. Well, I think we can. And I just can't bear to
see you marry someone else. Please call me, Jesse. Please.*
Nate

Okay.

How worried on a scale of 1–10 should I be about that letter,
which arrived a week ago?

I'm only asking because I basically pretended it didn't exist,
and right now, as a funny feeling grips my stomach, I'm beginning to wonder if that was the best tactic.

"I found it!" Laurel, my maid of honor rushed into the
room, holding my something old—a baseball card from my

209

dad's collection. She put it into the spot in my bouquet and surveyed me. "You look beautiful."

I peered down at my satin dress. I had never felt so good in anything. "I can't believe this is all really happening."

Just then Linda came into the room. "Okay, Jesse. Are you ready? Should I give the pianist the green light?"

I nodded, happy butterflies swarming in my stomach. "Let's do this!"

Uncle Logan came up beside me and held out his hand. "Here we go."

I took a deep breath as my bridesmaids, Laurel and Sarah, moved toward the doors that led to the chapel and then followed behind and waited at the end of the line, out of sight. As I stood there, all I could think about was walking toward my groom.

Finally I heard the music cue and the sound of the guests standing, and the ushers swung the doors open.

Logan squeezed my hand and escorted me down the aisle, every step moving me closer to the man I was going to marry.

When I reached his side, he held out his hand and whispered, "You look beautiful."

I basked in his love for a wonderful, warm moment, and then turned to face the minister.

"Jesse! Don't do it!"

Everyone in the room gasped as Nate ran down the aisle.

He stopped when he reached my side. "Jesse. You were the best thing that ever happened to me. Please don't do this."

Loud whispers echoed in the church, and the groomsmen looked at each other as if wondering what to do.

"I never stopped loving you," Nate continued. "I know you didn't want it to end. And I know I took a long time to realize it . . . But I didn't either. Jesse, please—"

Nate's voice was cut off by the loud smacking sound of my future husband punching him right in the jaw.

A few people screamed.

And as Nate cradled his jaw with his hand, I realized he really wasn't that good looking.

And he kind of smelled.

And when it came to kissing, he was pretty bad.

I mean, really, what did I ever see in that sack of—

"What is this?" I dropped the script pages on my lap.

Ethan smiled over at me. We were in the back seat of his car, eating mini-pancakes on the way to the wedding.

Our wedding!

And guess what day it was.

August 15th: National Creamsicle Day!

Yep. At the reception we were having a whole ice cream bar, complete with endless Creamsicles.

Does it get any better?

"What?" Ethan asked. "I thought he deserved to get punched."

"But there's no Nate in the rest of the story. He just shows up and tries to break up the wedding so Troy can punch him out."

"So?" Ethan shrugged. "I like it."

"And all that stuff he said in the letter . . ."

"It's what he's going to be thinking for the rest of his life."

I kissed my amazing, adorable groom's cheek and bit into another pancake.

Ethan was almost done with his sequel, *Troy Marries Girl*, and I'd found some idea notes on the floor of his car. That's what I was reading just now.

And guess what else I found on the floor of the car.

The offer letter I got six months ago from the Alive Academy of the Arts in Hill Pointe. Apparently, the person they hired was a dental assistant who could barely draw a circle. I accepted the offer, and I was loving my new job.

"Driver," I said, "could you turn up the music? I like this song."

"Just because I'm driving doesn't mean I'm a driver," David

grumbled from the front seat. And then he turned up the Sun Kil Moon song.

I rested my head on Ethan's shoulder and tried to memorize the moment.

The next little bit was a whirl—arriving at the church, listening to Laurel fight with the florist, slipping into my vintage tea-length silk dress with a lace overlay as Magda blew into a party kazoo, and watching as Sarah begged Conner to put his pants back on.

After what seemed like mere seconds, my mom—who arrived the night before the wedding via a VW bus driven by a guy named Zoltan—was poking her head into the Sunday School room and saying, "Showtime."

Laurel and Sarah, my bridesmaids, and Hayley, the flower girl, filed out. I followed behind and stood in my place at the back of the line.

Uncle Logan came to my side and took my hand and rested it on his arm. "Your dad would have been so proud," he said, his voice full of emotion.

"I think so," I said, feeling myself well up.

The tinkling sound of the piano signaled it was time to start, and the chapel doors swung open. I watched Hayley and Conner—who had put his pants on after being promised unlimited ice cream at the reception—step into the aisle, followed by Laurel and David and Sarah and Bill.

And then it was like time stopped.

I felt Logan squeeze my hand, and I moved forward, my shoes touching the aisle that would lead me to the rest of my life. I locked in on Ethan, and his eyes were filled with what I can only describe as adoration. When I got to his side, he reached for my hand, and it was like something clicked into place.

I was home.

A few beautiful moments later, I was no longer Ethan's fiancée. I was his wife. The minister held out his hands and announced us as a married couple, and the crowd stood and clapped.

As we waved out at them, Ethan whispered to me. "I just got another idea for the story."

I smiled and squeezed his hand as we ran up the aisle, all hitched and stuff.

"Me too."

Discussion Questions

1. Magda goes to great lengths to give Jesse a nudge into the dating world. Do you think any of her actions cross the line? Do you know anyone like Magda?
2. Jesse's dates with Ethan are fairly simple, and her dates with Troy are lavish. Do you think lavishness is necessary for romance? Why or why not?
3. Jesse says that in her time of sorrow, she found comfort in focusing outward. Do you think this works?
4. Throughout the book, Jesse keeps a secret. Do you feel she was right to keep this secret? Would you have done the same thing?
5. Was Nate justified in leaving?
6. Ethan is a struggling writer; Troy is a successful advertising executive. Do you think a steady job is a prerequisite for a potential mate?
7. When was the last time you had Spry gum?

About the
Author

Originally from California, Elodia Strain has lived every-where from Alaska to Washington to Pennsylvania, where *My Girlfriend's Boyfriend* is set. She currently makes her home near Dallas, Texas, where she loves playing with her adorable nieces and nephews, swimming, and enjoying good Tex-Mex.

Elodia is also the author of *The Icing on the Cake*, for which she was named Best New Fiction Author by Cedar Fort, and *Previously Engaged*, which was a 2009 Whitney Award Finalist. She can be found online at www.elodiastrain.com.